Off Switch

2

A Novel

By Kevin E Lake

Edited by Truman Jackson

Other Books Available by Kevin E Lake

1- Homeless Across America (non-fiction)

http://www.amazon.com/Homeless-Across-America-ebook/dp/B004HB2484/ref

2- Serial Street

http://www.amazon.com/Serial-Street-ebook/dp/B004HFRLPQ/ref

3- From the Graves of Babes *

http://www.amazon.com/From-Graves-Babes-ebook/dp/B004N62RU8/ref

4- Isle of Kapre

http://www.amazon.com/Isle-Kapre-Kevin-Lake-ebook/dp/B00DJXXC0A/ref

*Amazon's #1 ghost novel in customer satisfaction for six months in the year of its release!

This book is dedicated to every veteran from every war, past, present and future. And there will be more, for remember, 'only the dead have seen the end of war.'

It is especially dedicated to the 81'st HBCT with whom I deployed to Iraq as part of the Washington Army National Guard in 2008-09, for putting up with the suck.

Specifically, to my unit, A 2-146 Field Artillery of Montesano, WA and the 712'Th MP Company of the Texas Army National Guard who was attached to us, for putting up with the stupid.

In Memory

Specialist Samuel Donald Stone, age 20, from Port Orchard, WA, a machine gunner assigned to Troop C, 1st Squadron, 303rd Cavalry Regiment, a part of the 81st Brigade Combat Team, who died May 31st, 2009 as a result of a vehicle accident during a mounted combat logistical patrol near Tallil, Iraq.

Sergeant William Spencer, age 40, from Tacoma, WA, who passed away on February 25, 2010. Sergeant Spencer sustained a non-combat related injury in Iraq and was evacuated to Landstuhl Regional Medical Center in Germany where he later passed away.

Sergeant Jeremiah James Marsh, age 31, a Grayland, WA resident, Combat Veteran, Stafford Creek Correctional officer, Grayland Volunteer Firefighter, Fire Commissioner, and Defense Contractor who died tragically, Saturday morning, February 18, 2012 in an automobile accident on SR 105 in Grayland, WA, after serving his country with two deployments in the war on terror.

Specialist Stone and Sergeant Spencer were brothers in arms I never knew, but whose sacrifice I will always remember. Sergeant Marsh was my N.C.O., at times my truck commander while in Iraq, and always my friend who I will never forget.

United States Department of Veterans Affairs

Huntington Regional Office

676 Fifth Ave.
Huntington, WV 25801
Phone: 800-827-xxxx
Fax: 304-399-xxxx

Contents:

Transcript of Interview (April 11, 2010), re: internal review for potential disciplinary action against Jennifer Hutton, L.C.S.W.

Inquiries to be directed to the VA regional office in Huntington, West Virginia at the address listed above, or by telephone, fax or website.

*Text taken from audio transcript from third and final day of investigation:

INT: Miss Hutton, can you please explain how Mr. Prine came to possess your personal cell phone number in his cell phone?

SUBJ: I had called him before. To reschedule an appointment. I guess he saved the number.

INT: And can you explain, Miss Hutton, why you personally would call a patient, instead of having your assistant do it? And even then, why you would do it from a personal number instead of using the VA's telephone system?

SUBJ: I was in a hurry. I'm overloaded with cases. Sometimes it's quicker. More efficient to just do things myself instead of pass them on and hope they get done in a timely manner.

(A long pause before the next line of questioning)

INT: I'm going to play the recording of the phone call between you and Mr. Prine, just before… well. Listen please.

*From the audio recording of aforementioned phone call:

Jennifer Hutton (JH)-"Corey, where are you? What's going on?"

Corey Prine (CP)-"I've had enough."

JH- "Where are you? Corey, please."

CP- "I'm here. Outside."

JH- "Outside where?"

CP- "Outside of my body."

JH- "Corey. You are going through some badass withdrawal! Can you just sit tight until I get there? Are you somewhere safe?"

CP- "I'm so cold."

JH- "Are you outside? I hear the wind. God, Corey, where are you?"

CP- "I'm here."

JH- "Where is here?"

CP- "I can look down and see myself."

JH- "What do you see?"

CP- "I see myself."

JH- "And what do you look like?"

CP- "I don't look like me."

JH- "Why not, Corey?"

CP- "That's not my weapon."

JH- "What? Corey! Do you still have the gun?"

CP- "It's not my weapon. It's Emerson's."

JH- "Corey! Just stay exactly where you are until I get there!"

CP- "But they'll come for me. And I can't let them take me! And this isn't my weapon. It's Emerson's. I can see it. I'm right down there holding it. In the water."

JH- "Corey, please. Just listen to me."

CP "What do I do?" (Barely audible sobbing)

JH- "Corey." (a long pause in audio) "There is only one thing you can do."

CP- "What was that? The storm. I can't hear you. You're breaking up on me. What did you say?" (Barely audible mumbling follows- sounds like 'Damn, I'm …ooking up at my... With Emer…weap...')

JH- "There is only one thing you can do, Corey."

*Call ends here

INT: Can you explain, Miss Hutton, what it was, exactly, that you meant by, "There is only one thing you can do?"

1

*VA medical center computer notes of Jennifer Hutton, L.C.S.W.

August 12, 2009

Met this a.m. with new patient, Corey Prine. Prine is a twenty eight year old male, recently returned from deployment in Iraq. Mosul. Back for three months. Deployed with the Virginia Army National Guard. Claims to be doing an interstate transfer to a local guard unit here in West Virginia.

Patient appeared healthy. Eyes and skin clear. Demeanor and behavior adequate. Able to sit still and focus on conversation entire session. Un-common for so many vets suffering from PTSD, which Prine perhaps does, as indicated as a possibility in re-deployment notes from Army demobe station.

Currently, patient is living in apartment above his parent's garage in Summers County. Not working. Says he is taking time off after deployment. Claims to have very little money saved from either the deployment or from unspent leave, hence his current living situation. Considering college but unsure. Awaiting VA disability claim determination for PTSD and various physical injuries. Session lasted one hour. Scheduled Prine to return in 30 days.

*

*From the Personal diary (hand written in paper journal) of Jennifer Hutton

August 12, 2009

Dearest Diary,

Great workout at gym this evening after work. 30 minutes lifecycle, worked legs on nautilus, low weight high reps, 400 meter swim then 20 minutes in hot tub. I'm going to feel this one tomorrow.

Met with a new patient today; Corey Prine. My God did he give me the creeps! Good looking guy, well built, about ten years my junior, but God, *his eyes*.

There was something about his eyes.

Nice eyes, yes, but just… hard to explain. I felt like he was looking into my soul, almost reading my mind. I'm sure he has PTSD (who doesn't coming back, right?) but his seems to be manifesting in a different way than I am used to seeing, and I can tell.

He didn't fidget in his chair and rub his sweaty palms all over the arms like so many of my other vets. God I'm getting tired of disinfecting those damn chairs. He wasn't rude, obnoxious or loud. Nothing in his behavior was threatening. And that is what was so creepy.

I can tell he is angry. Very angry! It is in his eyes. But he seems to be able to hold it together. As if he's been back for years, but he's only been back a few months.

I have reason to believe this guy is smart. Very smart.In my fifteen years with the VA I don't think I've run across a vet quite like Corey. And this VA job's a joke too. Nothing compared to private practice, I'm told. And they only send me the lightweights. The real psychos get locked up right away in either Clarksburg or down in Salem, Virginia. If they even let them out of demobe that is.

But something about this guy. I found myself making a rookie mistake I haven't made in years. I was doing all the talking! I know I was nervous, and I know he could tell. He sat there, his legs crossed, resting his chin on his fist, just smirking while I waxed on and on. I sounded like that idiot I used to work with, Byron Blevins. I mean, I still have to deal with Blevins every now and then, with the guys I send to him for inpatient down in Salem, but that is better than when he worked here and I had to see him every day. Glad that didn't last long.

Anyway, with Corey just sitting there staring at me like that, well, it creeped me out and made me talk even more.

Ugh!!!!

He's coming back in a month, and by God I'll be ready for him. I hope. Gotta pull myself together with this one.

Anyway, Rob's been calling. I didn't return the calls. He is such a prick! A heartless prick! And he's being so with the wrong girl!

He knows how close to home his comments hit, because of how much I care for the vets that I work with. And he doesn't seem to give a flying fuck anyway! And then he wonders why I won't open up more with him. Really?

But my God is he a great lay! And a girl has her needs. God, give me the strength to use my head, not my heart….

Oh hell, heart shit! He's hot and I'm horny! Where's my cell phone?

Good night, dearest diary!!!

*

"FUCK! Why can't I sleep?" Corey Prine said aloud, sitting up in his bed.

Too many sounds; explosions, small arms fire, and that incessant humming in his ear, the one caused by the constant whine of the gun truck's engine.

He knew the sounds weren't really there, the bombs and the guns at least. But, by God, if he didn't hear them anyway every time he ALMOST fell asleep.

But the humming in the ear. That was real. Tinnitus they had told him it was at the demobe station in Georgia. He'd get ten percent disability from the VA for that alone, they'd said.

A whopping $127 a month.

But it was $127 a month for life, and tax free, so that really made it more like $135 a month for life. Just like the humming in his hear. Oh, but there were no tax advantages to the humming, it was just there for life.

They'd told him to keep a fan or an air conditioner running for background noise when he went to bed to drown out the hum so he could sleep. That was all well and good down there at the Army's demobe station in Georgia, but this late in the year in

West 'by God' Virginia the nights were just a little too cold for fans and air conditioners.

A lot too cold.

Freeze to death or die from some careless accident rooted in sleep deprivation. Just like all those gunners in Iraq, crushed to death when their drivers fell asleep at the wheel and flipped their gun trucks. These were his options.

"Fuck!"

And then there was the ever present pain in his lower back. The constant throbbing. And there was no position in which he could lay that would make it stop for more than just a few minutes. *But hey*, they'd told him, *he'd get some money for that too, b*ecause that was from all that body armor that he *had* to wear. Part of the uniform.

And not optional!

Like the earplugs and goggles and gloves and helmet and fire retardant uniforms. Get killed while not wearing any of it, even the ear plugs (ear plugs that didn't save you from tinnitus but made it damn near impossible to hear your battle buddies coming across on the headphones) and the D.O.D. would not pay your death benefit from your life insurance to your survivors, because everyone knew that a little pair of foam ear plugs would keep you from getting incinerated by a ten thousand pound dump truck bomb, right?

'Sorry, Ma'am,' Corey could hear all of those senior officers greeting all of those new widows at their doors saying. Widows who were barely out of their teens and senior officers who had never stepped foot in a combat zone. 'He would have made it. Wouldn't have been fried to a crisp if only he'd been wearing his little foam earplugs. But here, take this flag in lea of your $400,000 life insurance benefit.'

"Fuck!"

And then all the other thoughts, like his wife.

Ex-wife.

And *that little faggot from the bank*, as Corey thought of him that she started screwing the minute the plane lifted off, in route for hell ('must not be too much of a faggot if he's laying the pipe to your wife', his lieutenant, LT Bee had gone out of his way to tell him once word got around while in Iraq).

Truth be told, she'd planned on screwing him before the plane even took off, and Corey had known it. She hadn't been able to wait for Corey to deploy and get the hell out of her way.

And his truck, the one he spent weekends (at least the three weekends a month he hadn't had guard drill) cleaning with a fine toothed brush. It never looked any different than the day he had driven it off the lot. Even under the hood and after four years of use; backwoods, four-wheelin' and muddin' redneck use! The same truck the little faggot from the bank wrecked (no doubt on their way back from the club where they had been spending HIS money) while he was gone and that she later sold for pennies on the dollar instead of having fixed. She had pocketed the insurance money, and the little faggot had helped her spend it.

"Fuck!"

Speaking of, don't forget about the money. She'd draw it out every other week, like clockwork, when the good 'ol army put it in their joint account. Once they'd actually started paying him four months into the deployment that was. What a story there, a soldier in Iraq not receiving pay and no one doing jack shit about it. *That was all that damn LT Bee's fault too,* he thought.

But when they *had* started paying him, he'd gone through his chain of command, making it all the way up to his C.O. (Company Commanding Officer) about his wife cleaning him out back home and the C.O. had told him to 'keep his head in the game.' And that 'if it's a joint account there is nothing any of us can do.'

"Fuck!"

But most of all, don't *even* bring up his son, who would be one year, six months and five days old now (he kept count to the day) and who wouldn't recognize him from Adam. His son had only been three months old when he deployed and he had not seen him since.

"Fuck!"

From 'PTSD Nation – The New 'ism for a New Generation' (pp. 3-4) by Jerry Barnes, Ph.D., Ed.D., former M.D.

"By most in the mental health industry (yes, Good Reader, it is now an industry, whored out and profited from as much as any company creating 'widgets' for sale) Post Traumatic Stress Disorder(P.T.S.D.) is defined as a severe anxiety disorder that can develop after exposure to any event that results in psychological trauma. This event may involve the threat of death to oneself or to someone else, or to one's own or someone else's physical, sexual, or psychological integrity, overwhelming the individual's ability to cope.

In our society, the 'ism of P.T.S.D. is graciously awarded to rape victims, survivors of automobile accidents, and to so many of our military veterans coming back from the wars in the Middle East who have been shot, blown up, or who have witnessed others being shot or blown up. Etc.

But pay close attention to the part of the definition that mentions threat to one's own or another's personal integrity. Individuals who have experienced this part of the definition *only* are not so gloriously awarded the 'ism.

In regard to our military personnel, such examples of 'threat to psychological integrity' runs a very wide gamut from abusive leadership within the ranks to advantages being taken upon the service member while they are serving overseas, by civilians back home, such as spouses cleaning out bank accounts, committing adultery, damaging or selling the service members personal property, alienating the service member from their children or other family members, etc.

It is assumed by many people, far too many, that if the negative experience did not involve physical pain or an external threat to one's life (PLEASE pay attention to the word 'external' here. This will be addressed at length later in the suicide section of this work) then the candidate is not worthy of the 'ism. This almost ALWAYS leads to further feelings of alienation by those suffering, compounding their feelings of hopelessness and despair, and diminishing, even further, their ability to cope.

2

*Meeting between Jennifer Hutton and Corey Prine - September 12, 2009

"So, Corey," Jennifer said, flashing a friendly, beautiful smile. "How are we today?"

Corey found her a breath of fresh air compared to the ugly, snapping jowls of his former military leadership. Her sky blue eyes gave a feeling of peace, and her long chestnut hair flowed like the calming waters of a mountain stream. She wore little make up, but little was needed. Corey thought she was naturally beautiful.

"This part of *we* is fine," he said. "How is your part of *we*, Ms. Hutton?"

"Oh, call me Jennifer," she said, waving her hand and rolling her eyes. "You're not at drill or on deployment."

"And thank God for that," he said, almost smiling.

"Do you miss the environment?" She squinted while simultaneously raising her eyebrows. The 'I really care' look former President Bill Clinton had made famous from the backwoods of Arkansas all the way to the White House.

"Hell no," he said, no hesitation.

"You may miss it in time, believe it or not. Don't fight the feelings if and when they come. It's all part of the healing process."

Oh shit, I'm talking too much again, she thought.

"So what did you do in the Army, Corey?"

Nice recovery, Jen, she thought. *Always use their names. It's warm and fuzzy. God, why does this guy make me feel like a freshman in psych 101?*

"Well *Jennifer*. I was an airborne infantryman," he said.

She wasn't sure if his tone was one of pride or sarcasm. Again, she felt that he was reading her mind, her motives. He crossed his legs and folded his hands over his lap, mimicking her position.

"So in Iraq, did you jump out of planes? Is it ok if I ask you about your experiences in Iraq?"

"Sure," he said. "That's why I'm here, isn't it?" He smiled this time, but only with his mouth. It was the smile of a man angry on the inside. The mouth lies but not the eyes. *Never* the eyes.

Those eyes.

"And no. I didn't jump out of planes in Iraq."

"So what did you do while you were there? What was your job? Your mission as you guys call it?"

"I wasted a year of my life hauling water around from place to place and putting up with stupid shit from a bunch of fucking retards."

"Wow!" she said.

Keep it up Jen, she thought. *You're getting somewhere with this one.*

"What exactly does that mean though?" she asked.

"I was a machine gunner for a convoy security team that provided protection for the trucks hauling our drinking water around the northern part of that shit hole you people back here know as Iraq. We'd pick it up at the source. Some sink hole filled with this shitty colored water in Mosul and then truck it about two hours south. That's where it was purified and bottled. Then we'd deliver palettes of it to all our little bases scattered throughout the north."

He paused. She remained silent.

He (or she) who speaks first loses, she thought.

"I rode around in a truck, wearing 40 pounds of body armor and ammo in one hundred and thirty degrees heat for a year, getting shot at and blown up for water. Not so much oil,ya see."

Yes! she thought. *Score one for Jennifer! You've got him talking!*

"So you feel as if your time there was wasted?" she said.

Leading the patient your honor.

"Wouldn't you? I'm a trained killer, not a water boy."

"What do you mean by, you're a trained killer?"

"Look," he said, uncrossing his legs and leaning forward. "I was trained to kick in doors. Shoot people in the face. I was desensitized to the act of taking another human being's life. All this at basic training at Ft. Benning, Georgia. Then, on top of that, I was motivated to kill! We dreamed about it. Fantasized about it. *We* here not being you and me, Jennifer, but me and the other infantryman I trained and served with." He sat back in his chair, as if realizing he was saying too much too soon. "Then they send us over there to be water boys."

"Why do you think you were sent to transport water?" she asked. "I've never served in the Army, but my dad did. And I've worked with so many vets for so long that I am familiar with what you call, M. O. S (Military occupational service). I mean, aren't there some non-combat arms units that could haul water? Let you guys go weed out the bad guys?"

"Yes," he said, re-crossing his legs, relaxing. "Eighty eight mikes- transportation. The problem was that by the time we got to theater in 2008, we were *all* eighty eight mikes. The war was over. It had *been* over. We were well into the occupation by then. Didn't seem there were any terrorists left to fight."

"So who was shooting at you? Blowing you up?"

"Locals," he said and then waved a dismissive hand. "Everyone wanted their claim to fame that they were fighting the occupiers. Once a week or so we'd take fire. Some kid with his dead daddy's AK-47 would take a couple pop shots from a roof top as we rolled through their village and then run for the damn hills like cowards."

"Did you ever fire back?"

"Oh hell no!" he said, uncrossing his legs and sitting forward again. "I didn't want to go to prison!"

"What?"

"The R.O.E. (rules of engagement) was strict as hell while we were there. If you fired a round you'd at least lose rank and pay. If you hit someone? Jail time! No questions asked. 'The unnecessary discharge of a weapon' they called it."

"So do you feel as if you were sent there without the right to defend yourself?"

Wow Jen, you're knocking this one out of the park. Keep him talking. Keep him talking.

"No," he said, looking up and laughing. It was a genuine laugh. He even engaged his eyes this time. "Those fucktards couldn't aim. And I knew the rules were set as they were 'cause the brass knew the war was over. It had moved from the deserts of Iraq to the aisles of Congress. "

"What about the roadside bombs? Who was putting those out?"

"Same people. Locals. But they weren't really trying to hit us. Oh hell no! They'd learned early. You blow up a truck, we take out a village.

"No, the actual bomb makers would pay the locals to place the bombs for them, while they high-tailed their sorry asses back across the boarders into Syria or Iran. Hell, even southern Turkey at times. The locals needed the money the insurgents paid them, so they took it. But they'd place the bombs, usually in big white rice sacks, right in the middle of the road at the end of a long straight so we'd see them in time. Only one hit our truck while I was there. It sounded like a damn fire cracker it was so small. It cracked the passenger side mirror. That's all."

"Wow," she said, sounding astonished, though she had been hearing this same story from different vets for at least two years now. "Sounds like both sides knew it was an occupation by the time you were there and were just waiting for it to end."

"Yep," he said, extending his legs and crossing his hands over his lap. He looked down at his toes. He was relaxed. Getting it out, some of it anyway, was working. "Everyone was just sitting around waiting for the assholes in D.C. to quit sucking all that contractor cock. Make enough money to spare some lives on both sides." He took a long pause. "And damn was it hot over there while we were waiting."

Another long pause ensued, a lengthy silence. Not a 'he (or she) who speaks first loses' silence, but a healing silence. Jennifer knew this and honored it. Corey was finding peace, rather, peace was finding Corey.

After nearly a minute, Jennifer said, "Corey? Can we talk for just a little bit about life now that you're back?"

Never let them leave focusing on the war, Jen.

"Huh?" he said, coming out of his trance, looking around the room as if awakening from a dream. "Oh, sure. Sure."

"What have you been doing with yourself? How are you spending your time now that you're back? Have you thought about finding a job?"

"Oh yeah," he said, completely re-engaged. "I even went looking."

"Great!"

Man I wish all my vets could jump back into the saddle like this guy.

"Where did you go? How did it turn out?"

"Do you know the pallet plant over in Hinton?"

"Yeah," she said. "I have some vets that work there."

"I worked there in the summers during high school. I went there. Thought maybe I'd walk right into a spot with my time served in Iraq and all."

"And?"

"And it was weird."

"How so?"

"Well, the same manager was still there from when I worked there before, Jesus, it must be twelve years ago now, Dave Lupshin. He really seemed glad to see me again.

"He hadn't heard that I was in Iraq. He didn't know what had happened to me after I left the state with…" He squirmed a bit in his seat. "With April. After high school."

The ex-wife. He isn't ready for this yet Jen. Don't push him, she thought.

"Anyway, after I brought him up to speed, he was telling me a spot was open on receiving. Unloading the trucks that come in. You know, they don't make anything there. They just get pallets from all over, tear them apart and sell the refuse."

Jennifer nodded in understanding.

"So, he asks me if I'm out of the guards yet," Corey continued. "I told him I was doing an interstate transfer into the local unit. That I had 90 days to do it and my time was about up, but I was taking every damn day of it I could so I wouldn't have to go to drill for a while. I have two years left in the guard, ya know.

"Then he told me he'd heard the local unit was deploying to Afghanistan next spring. Said they'd come back from Iraq a few years ago, and they were due to go back to the Middle East. I told him I hadn't heard. I hadn't made it my business to find out, ya know. My mind's still a little pre-occupied with the last deployment."

Jennifer shook her head again. She was following.

"Well, he left for a little while. Left me sitting there in the break room. When he came back in, he told me he'd been wrong and that there were no openings, but that he'd keep me in mind. He shook my hand, thanked me for my service, and then he sent me on my way as if he really *wasn't* so happy to see me anymore."

"Do you believe him, Corey?" Jennifer said. "That there really were no openings?"

"I did at first. But a week later, I was eating dinner with mom and dad, and they told me my cousin Joey had gotten a job at the pallet mill that day. The day we were eating that is. He's started already. I guess maybe something came open and Dave *hadn't* kept me in mind."

"Do you really think that's what happened, Corey?"

"I have no evidence that things happened for any other reason."

"Is your cousin in the guard or reserves?" she asked.

"Oh hell no," Corey said, chuckling. "That fatass bastard couldn't get through the first week of basic training. I hope they don't have him doing too much physical labor down there at the plant. It's liable to kill him. And he's only twenty three years old. Sad really.

"You know?" he said, almost as an afterthought. "I'm really kinda glad I didn't get that job anyway."

"Why is that?" Jennifer asked, tilting her head sideways and squinting.

"I was leaving the lot. I'd walked there, see, 'cause my driver's license expired while I was in Iraq. I haven't been in a big hurry to get it renewed because Hinton is so small you can walk from one end of town to the other in five minutes. And I ride the VA van for free to my appointments here in Beckley.

"But while I was leaving the plant, I had my head down and an empty semi was coming up from behind me. It was bouncing around in the lot and I could hear the big chains they use to strap loads down with bangin' and clangin' around on the metal of the truck bed. It was the exact same sound our gun trucks would make in the motor pool on our way off the base, heading out of the gate for mission. And goddamn! I was right back there in the motor pool again. In my head. But it seemed so real! I was right back in Iraq!"

Jennifer looked at him, her heart not breaking but certainly bending.

This is the part they don't get, she thought. 'They' being those who haven't been where Corey and other vets like him have been. It wasn't just loud noises like cars backfiring that brought it back. There was so much that opened the doors of the house of pain that sat on that large plot of land inside their subconscious minds.

Other sounds, like Corey's semi coming through a lot could bring it all back instantly. It could be odors. One of her vets couldn't stand getting within a mile of a Red Lobster. 'We were served steak and lobster every Sunday in the chow hall,' he had told her. 'Nice touch, yes. And we loved it. But now, every time I smell lobster, BAM! I'm right back in Iraq.'

"Will this pass, too?" Corey asked. His heart rate had risen while he had told the story, but it was slowing now. His forehead glistened with a light coat of sweat.

"I could win you over by lying to you Corey, but I have too much respect for you and the things you've done to do that. No. It won't. There will always be sounds, smells, experiences you go through that will bring it back."

"Oh," he said, looking down. "Thanks for your honesty."

"We can't make these things go away, Corey. But we can work on dealing with them. That's why I'm here, and that is why I want you to keep coming back."

"Sure," he said, sensing the session was over. "Want me back in another month, Doc?"

He smiled. It was a forced smile. He tried to engage his eyes but his efforts were futile. Jennifer could tell that he was helping her help him as much as he could. She could tell that he wanted to get better.

"I'm not a Doc, Corey. Just a social worker."

"You will be someday," he said.

It wasn't the first time she'd heard it.

*

*From the personal diary of Jennifer Hutton – September 12, 2009

Dearest Diary,

I had a great day today! Made major headway with Corey Prine. I almost feel guilty for the feelings I had about him previously.

He finally opened up and started talking. He told me about his time in Iraq. At least a little.

But I'm not scared of him anymore. There is still something there I can't quite put my finger on. Anger? Extreme anger? Not so sure what it is but after today I know I can work with him.

He is smart, like I suspected. He's able to see the bullshit going on in the world in a light most of these guys can't, because they've drank too much of the defense department's kool-aid. Well, except for maybe all the bullshit he's going to have to put up with here at home, like trying to find a job while he's still in the guard and deployable.

But still, it was a great session and I'm in a good mood. In such a good mood that I actually returned Rob's call. I'm going to dinner with him at Garfield's at Cross Roads Mall. God I miss Seattle so much sometimes, like when I'd *really* like to go somewhere nice and eat.

Oh, and I'm writing in you early this evening, Dearest Diary, because if things go well I won't be sleeping with *you* tonight!

Good night, Dearest Diary.

★

"Well, you seem perky this evening," Rob said, rising to greet Jennifer as she walked into the restaurant. "Good day?"

"Yes," she said, matter-of-factly. "Good day indeed."

"Don't have too many of those, putting up with all those whiners. Definitely cause for celebration," he said, sitting again and tipping his beer to her before taking a drink. He'd gotten there an hour early and had polished off three beers already, like he usually did.

"If you are going to start that shit already, I'm leaving now," she said, still standing.

"Sorry, Jen," he said, rising again. "Sorry. I really am."

They both sat down.

"So, it's been a while. How have you been?" he said.

"Rob, it's been a week."

"I know, but it feels like it's been longer." He motioned the waitress to bring menus, the waitress he'd been flirting heavily with before Jennifer's arrival. Jennifer ordered a diet coke as the waitress dropped off the menus, and Rob ordered another beer. "I've missed you."

Jennifer and Rob had never been steady for any extended period of time, though they'd been seeing each other for years. On again off again from the beginning.

She didn't mind that he was divorced with two kids. Who wasn't this day and age by their late thirties other than her, she'd often thought.

Their problems revolved around cultural differences. Jennifer was a west coast girl, born, raised, and educated in Seattle. She had come to West Virginia fifteen years earlier to take a position with the VA, a position that she viewed at the time as temporary.

Being that those days were during peace time, she wasn't too busy at first and had thoughts of chasing that illustrious Ph.D. (which in the past several years she had come to believe really *did* stand for 'piled higher and deeper').

But the customers would soon come knocking as those first to deploy to the Middle East after September 11 started coming home. Back from either front; Afghanistan first, then soon following, Iraq.

She'd developed relationships, professional and clinical, with co-workers and patients, and she didn't feel as if she could just bail on any of them to chase that deeply stacked pile of academic feces. Nor to follow up on the other thoughts that often crossed her mind; returning to the Pacific Northwest, where, in spite of the rain, she was more comfortable, and for her, things just seemed to make more sense.

She had been physically attracted to Rob from the first time she had laid eyes on him. He had been working at the VA himself at the time, doing intake at the E.R. He had pulled eight years in the Army, making his way up to staff sergeant before deciding not to re-enlist when his contract was up just after the attacks of September 11. 'Eight years are enough,' he'd tell anyone when asked why he hadn't re-enlisted.

Rob didn't particularly care for what he referred to as the 'cry baby attitudes' of the vets coming back from the fronts. He missed his own days of service when he could give simple answers to soldiers for their problems. Answers like, 'suck it up and drive on,' or, 'just kill yourself now and get it over with.' These statements were definite no-no's at the VA, so in good conscience, and at the urging of his superiors, he moved on.

He'd been working at the Department of Motor Vehicles (DMV) ever since, and he liked it. Still government work with arguably decent pay (you could live on it) and great bennies. And a lot less 'cry babies.'

Aside from their cultural differences, Jennifer could never get past Rob's attitude toward the men and women of the armed forces for whom she cared so much. He had been married at the time when they first met, so it wasn't like any of it had mattered.

But a few years later, and after he had entered into divorce, Rob had re-initiated contact with Jennifer. They'd gone out for coffee and lunch together for months, and the day Rob's divorce was final, they consummated their own relationship with three hours in the sack, releasing month's worth of pent up sexual frustration they'd held toward each other.

And they'd been on again, off again ever since.

She enjoyed the way he opened doors for her like a true southern gentleman, but she hated how he didn't respect her views and opinions, like the men on the west coast seemed to do more, as if her gender made her less of a person.

But the sex? *'Jesus effin' Christ!'* she'd tell her friends, just before following with, 'those west coast pansies just can't move their asses like these good 'ol country boys.' She'd say it with her best twang, and after fifteen years in the mountain state, her twang had gotten good.

'I'm such a dirty whore,' she'd tell her diary in secret manuscripts, even though she wasn't. She wasn't even promiscuous. She enjoyed monogamy with Rob, and to her best knowledge, Rob was monogamous with her (but not for a lack of trying otherwise).

But if only he were a little different, she thought. If only she could change him.

What was the old expression she often thought of? Women settle down with men hoping they will change, and men settle down with women hoping they won't?

If only Rob were as good in other areas as he was in bed, she thought. Of course, after more than half a dozen years of on again, off again, he hadn't changed and she knew that he wasn't going to.

But at least there was the sex.

"So have you missed me enough to keep your feet out of your mouth for at least the amount of time it takes us to eat?" she asked and then took a sip of her diet coke.

"Yes," he said and then took another swig of beer. "So tell me about it."

"Why? So you can shoot some holes in my happiness? I tell you about making some headway with a new patient and you call him a whiner and I get mad and throw my drink in your face?"

"Ok," he said, waving a hand. "Let's start over. Jennifer, I've missed you. Work's fine. The kids are great (*but their mom's still a dirty bitch*- is what he usually said but left out this time) and the only thing missing to make my life complete has been you."

"That's better," she said, her smile returning. "I've been good too. And I'll admit, I've thought about you." She gave him her best sexy eyes.

"Really?" He laughed. "How often?"

"That's a secret."

They both laughed.

She ordered pasta, and he ordered ribs and three more beers. They ate dinner and then they went back to his place and were on again for the night.

*

Down in Hinton, in the small apartment above his parent's garage, Corey Prine was squeezing both sides of his head with the palms of his hands trying to hold his brains in. Metallica's, 'Until it Sleeps' was blaring from his speakers.

Why can't I fucking sleep!

The heavy metal wasn't helping but he had given up hope an hour before anyway.

God I wish I could call Emerson, he thought. It was after midnight, and too many thoughts kept him awake. That and the ringing in his ear and the throbbing in his lower back. But tonight, the thoughts took precedence over the pain.

That fucking whore! His ex-wife, who had run off with his son during the deployment.

His son, *one year, seven months and eight days old now.*

That fucking faggot! He'd run off with his wife (*ex-wife Corey*) and his son to some location, unbeknownst to him, on the west coast, so he'd heard. At least that is what that '*bitch whore's bitch of a mother*' had told him when he'd gone to her house after getting back from Iraq, just before she'd threatened a call to the police and a restraining order if he were to ever come by again.

But he couldn't call Emerson, because Emerson was dead. Emerson, his team leader, truck commander and friend.

It's all that goddamn LT Bee's fault! Corey thought.

Sgt. Emerson had always been everyone's 'go to guy' in time of need. But when Sgt. Emerson had needed help while in Iraq, he had chosen to go to the wrong guy.

'Soldier up Sergeant!' Lieutenant Bee had told him when Emerson approached him about problems back home. His wife was screwing his best friend and cleaning out his bank. '*Join the crowd, Emerson. You have all these soldiers under you sergeant! Set the example!*'

Emerson had been a hell of a soldier and a hell of an NCO (non-commissioned officer). But he was still only twenty two years old and vulnerable.

And human.

And he didn't want to talk about his problems back home with the soldiers under him. He *wanted* to continue being the 'go to guy' that he knew he was for them, so he had gone to LT Bee instead, taking it up the chain of command.

'You know what to do,' LT Bee had said, just before Emerson went back to his CHU (company housing unit- soldiers living quarters) and ate a bullet from his M-4 carbine.

Sixty days later the Army had called it, "Death from accidental discharge of personal weapon," after their investigation; an investigation that, for some reason, didn't involve questioning *anyone* in Emerson's platoon, like *all* the other investigations going on at the time for the same reasons.

Mass soldier suicide.

The suicide rate for those serving in the Middle East and those who had returned from serving in the Middle East had recently surpassed the suicide rate of civilians at the time, and for the first time in U.S. history, so the D.O.D. had gotten good at throwing the word 'accidental' around. Keep the numbers, and questions, down.

Goddamn you Emerson! I fucking need you! You know what this shit is like!

Emerson wasn't there, so Corey just stared at the wall, alone with his thoughts. The wall was beige in color but he saw it in a light shade of red, closer to pink, just like every night since coming home. But it was getting darker, becoming crimson.

Metallica's, 'Until it Sleeps' blared on.

*

From 'PTSD Nation – The New 'ism for a New Generation' (pp. 12-13) by Jerry Barnes, Ph.D., Ed.D., former M.D.

"…and the differences between the glamorized, romanticized images of war on the big screen and the grim realities of war in real life go farther than just the battle field. They come to the home front before, during, and after a service member's deployment. Let's study, for example's purpose, this concept of… no, this scream it from the hilltops mantra of "Support the Troops!"

This seems, in reality, to be nothing more than a nice catch phrase or slogan in which the bumper sticker companies of the world (which, Good Reader, I can assure you have been outsourced to the third world) are making money. Are people actually practicing this concept of 'supporting the troops?' More so than by simply slapping a bumper sticker on their vehicles? Those large, gas guzzling, monstrous sport utility vehicles, 95% of which never leave hard top or even have their four wheel drive mechanisms engaged?

Let's look at a common case for an unemployed National Guard soldier up for deployment within the next year. How many employers are willing to "support that troop?" Very few and here is why.

Through the Service Members Civil Relief Act, the US Government has mandated that if a company has an employee who is a member of the armed services, and that employee is to deploy, then the employer must hold that position for the employee for when (not to mention 'if') they return. They can fill the position with a temp, but it must be given back to the service member upon their return from deployment.

Now, knowing this, who wants to hire a guardsman or member of the reserves when the entire community knows that a deployment of the local unit is in the near future?

You don't believe me? Don't take my word for it. Google it, Good Reader. Find the numerous stories of our men and women in the guard and reserves who cannot find work for this very reason.

Now, we all know that employers cannot 'openly' discriminate against members of the armed services, the key word here, being 'openly,' anymore than employers can 'openly' discriminate against gays, blacks, ethnic minorities, or people with religious views different from their own.

Oh sure, in their 'infinite wisdom' our politicians have made it appear as if they are supporting our troops with this legislation. But in reality, it has done nothing more than gotten many of those politicians who pushed for this law re-elected, while the few who have stepped up to protect the many find themselves in the unemployment and welfare lines.

Think of this, Good Reader, the next time you want to add another "Support the Troops" sticker to your gas guzzler.

Oh, and lest we forget, those stickers are made from petroleum products.

3

*Meeting between Jennifer Hutton and Corey Prine at Beckley VA Medical Center October 9, 2009

"So, how are we today, Corey?"

"This part of *we* is good. How is your part of *we*?"

"Got me again," she said, laughing. "Seriously, how ya doing?"

She tried to say 'ya' as much as she could rather than the 'you' she had been saying all those years before moving to Appalachia. When in Rome…

"I'm good, I guess," he said, not so guarded as the first time they'd met.

"What do you mean, 'you guess?'"

"I'm tired a lot," he said. "I can't sleep at night."

"I saw in your records that you have filed a claim for tinnitus. Does the ringing in your ears keep you up?"

"Yeah."

"Anything else?"

He was quiet for a long, slow three count. "Not really."

"Corey," she said, drawing out the last syllable of his name as if he were a kid caught in the cookie jar. "Tell me what 'not really' means. This isn't my first day on the job, ya know."

Good Jen, she thought. *Another 'ya.'*

"Well," he said, hesitating. "I hear shit that's not there."

"Like what?"

"Gun shots, explosions. That kinda stuff."

"You told me about the small arms fire and the road side bombs in Iraq, Corey. Was there anything else? Car bombs? Mortars?"

"Oh hell yeah," he said, becoming adamant. "Hell, we got mortared every damn day. We worked at night see, because there was a curfew on the locals. They weren't allowed to drive between ten p.m. and four a.m. That helped us minimize the threat of SVBIEDS (suicide vehicle borne improvised explosive devices- in English, car bombs). So when we were trying to sleep during the day, they mortared the shit out of us. God, it was hard to sleep."

"So was it like that all year? You couldn't get any sleep?"

"No, not really. I mean, the mortars were there all year, but after a month or so we started sleeping."

"Just got used to the noise, huh?"

"Oh no," he said. "You can never get used to that. We'd just all go over to see Dr. Feelgood."

"And who was Dr. Feelgood?" Kid in the cookie jar again.

"Oh, he was one of many people. Some doctors that couldn't make it in private practice. These guys join the Army as

Lieutenant Colonels and for a big sign-on bonus, and then hand out drugs in Iraq and Afghanistan like candy. We'd go there for sleeping pills, and they worked."

"Do you remember the name of these sleeping pills?"

"Oh yeah. Klonopin. Still have some left over."

'Oh shit! Klonopin!' is what she thought, but what she said was, "Oh, Klonopin. Have you taken any since you've been back? On the nights you can't sleep?"

"Oh hell no!"

Oh thank God! she *thought.*

"And why not?" she said. "Does it not work for you anymore?"

"Oh it works. The shit's like a horse tranquilizer. I mean it knocks you the fuck out! But man, I've never had a hangover from a night out like that shit gives me. Not that it was a strong hangover, it just lasted all day. Till I took more Klonopin. And when I got off the stuff? Oh my God, what a trip *that* was!"

"I'm glad you're not taking that anymore, Corey. I'm not a big fan of meds myself. That's why I've not pushed myself for the med degree and the ability to prescribe, but there are definitely some meds that are worse than others, and Klonopin is about as bad as they get in the sleeping pills category."

"Then why do they give it to us in theater?"

"Why do you think? You're a smart guy."

"Because it works and it's cheap? Just like everything else the Army uses. The contract always goes to the lowest bidder?"

"You said it, not me," she said. "The VA's not too far removed from the D.O.D. when you start bad mouthing big brother, so there is only so much I can say. That's why I love working with you. You are smart enough to read between the lines."

There you, I mean, 'ya' go Jen, she thought. *Compliment, compliment, compliment. God this job is too much like sales.*

"Well, I know I'd rather fight insomnia than deal with that devil again," he said.

"You claimed before, Corey, that you don't drink alcohol or use any illicit substances. Is that still the case?"

"So far," he said, laughing. "I used to drink some in school with the guys up the holler on a huntin' trip or on the river fishin' but never too much. Got out of it after high school. Oh, I liked it. That's why I stopped. I think I liked it a little too much. I read the writing on the wall early I guess, that if I didn't stop I might not be able to at some point. But I'll admit, there are times when I'm tempted to just drink myself to sleep."

"Please don't do that, Corey. Your self-insight is wonderful. I wish everyone had it. Too many vets mess around with drugs and alcohol until they can't get off of it. I find too often with vets who start using, especially those with PTSD, get hooked too easily and give themselves a slew of new beasts to have to slay, other than just PTSD. A whole new set of problems."

"So what do I do? Will this pass?"

"It will," she said. "In time. I know it is hard to do, but you just have to be patient."

A period of silence passed between them.

"How have you been keeping yourself busy?" she asked. "Have you looked for any more jobs?"

"No," he said, looking down. "There's not anything around Hinton, really, other than the pallet plant, and, well, we know what happened there. I've been thinking about renewing my driver's license though and looking for something here in Beckley."

"You know, it's not just Hinton or other small towns scattered throughout the rust belt anymore," she said. "It's hard to find work anywhere in the country now."

"I know," Corey said. "We'd watch the news on the big screens in the chow halls. Try to keep up with stuff back home.

We watched the stock market crash and the government bail out the banks while forcing the home owners out on the streets 'cause they couldn't pay their mortgages. As weird as it sounds, it all made us happy to be there in a way. At least we had jobs for the time being."

"It's not weird at all, Corey. It's been rough over here. No one has any money."

"And you know what?" he said, smiling. "We are spending one million dollars a week just in soda pop and Gatorade for soldiers in Iraq and Afghanistan."

"No way!" she said, eyes wide. "I knew there were some pretty ridiculous ways we were spending money over there, but I'd never heard that one."

"Oh yeah," he said, chuckling. "Don't get me wrong. I mean, I drank my fair share of blue Gatorade over there. Loved it cold from the chow halls. I'd have one with my meal and take two to go as I was leaving."

He paused again, looking down. Jennifer recognized it as a healing pause and remained silent.

"I haven't been able to drink Gatorade since I came home," he finally said.

"You mentioned trying to find work here in Beckley," she said, but only after giving peace a little more time to comfort him. "Do you have transportation?"

My truck! My fucking truck, he thought.

"Are you okay, Corey?" She had seen the change in his expression, the flare in his eyes. His face had flushed red.

"Oh, yeah," he said, going back to white and bright as if the thought had never entered his mind. "No, I don't have a car. But mom told me I could use hers until I was able to get one."

"Sounds like your parents are supportive."

"They are," he said. "They pretty much stay out of my way and I stay out of theirs. I do it because I feel like a loser living at home at my age. They do it because I think they are afraid I'm bat shit crazy and am going to go off anytime." He threw his head back in laughter, almost maniacal laughter. "But it's all good for now."

"So how have you been staying busy with all that free time?" she asked.

"I haven't been, really. I mean, I read a lot and watch a lot of movies."

"Are you getting out and socializing?"

"Not really."

"And why not? Afraid to be around people? Crowds?"

"Like there are any crowds in Hinton," he said, and then laughed sarcastically. "Yeah, I'll admit, I avoid the Wal-Marts of the world, but that isn't really it."

"What is it?"

"The stupid questions. Always the same. 'How many people did you kill?' Shit like that."

"Isn't it hard to believe that there are people out there who actually ask that question of vets?" she said, genuinely frustrated. "It's like they think people join the military for the sole purpose of killing others. I mean, what a way to bring back a terrible memory for those who have."

"Yeah, and *you* know I didn't kill anyone. But try telling *them* that," he said, waving his arm in a wide sweep so as to include all of the people in the whole wide world outside of the office in which he and Jennifer now sat.

"I mean, you tell them that and they don't believe you," he said. "So I started saying 'yeah.'

"'How many?' they'd say.

"'One' I'd tell them. Then they'd crinkle their ugly, hillbilly faces and say, 'Is that all?'

"So I started saying three. Then four. Same thing. They still give you that stupid, disappointed look and say, 'Is that all?' But I finally figured out how to answer that moronic question. I'll share it with you. You might want to share it with some of your other vets."

"And what is the answer, Corey? How do you *possibly* give an answer to a question that stupid to satisfy the morbid curiosity of the disrespectful people who would ask it?"

"I tell them seventeen, and they look at me like I'm the monster they'd hoped I was and then they walk away in disgust and never fucking talk to me again!"

*

* VA computer system notes from Jennifer Hutton –

October 9, 2009

Making more progress with Corey Prine. He has really opened up over the past few months. He claims to currently be experiencing insomnia.

He is reclusive. Not so much afraid of, or uncomfortable around groups, but shows dislike toward individuals he feels are disrespectful toward him and insensitive in regard to his service.

Claims not to be using drugs of any kind, or alcohol, though admitted to taking Klonopin, as prescribed, while in Iraq. Experienced hallucinations during withdrawal from the drug when discontinuing use. Have scheduled him again for next month.

*

* Personal diary entry of Jennifer Hutton - October 9, 2009

Dearest Diary,

I screwed up today with Corey Prine! I've been screwing up with him for months and I just caught my mistake today. Shit!

Then, I screwed up again by bringing it up with Rob. Why do I even waste my time with him?

Anyway, I completely missed something with Corey. Something big! I went back through his intake questionnaire forms after he left today, which I have not been doing. He has really opened up and gotten good at sharing everything with me. At least I thought.

I was looking to see if he was still answering 'no' to the alcohol and drug questions because he claimed during our session that he didn't drink or use drugs. It came up because we were talking about the Klonopin he took while in Iraq. Yes, Dearest Diary, the same Klonopin tens of thousands of soldiers are taking just before going out with loaded .50 cals and grenade launchers. I hope the man behind the curtain, the one with the button,isn't on that shit! It's crack for insomniacs!

Anyway, on the 'Do you feel like hurting yourself or others' question, he'd answered 'yes.' And he's been answering yes the three months I've been seeing him!

God what a rookie mistake!

I'm just lucky to still have a job! If he'd have gone out and killed himself, or someone else, and I was not notating that I was addressing this issue? God, I'd end up like poor old Dr. Barnes.

Gee, I haven't visited that old ghost in a while.

Anyway, I need to have him back ASAP and bring this up. I'll think of something. Make it look like he scheduled earlier or something. Those bastards at the VA are always reading my notes, hence only my most intimate thoughts in regard to so many of my vets shared with you, Dearest Diary. I don't want to end up like Dr. Barnes.

Why do I feel that a visit to him is in order soon? Hell, it's time better spent than with Rob. What a jerk! When I brought all this up with him I got the same old shit I always get from him. 'Those whiners should just kill themselves.'

And he knows about my dad, or at least what I have vaguely suspected about my dad at times.

What an insensitive bastard!

But what's a girl to do when she simply needs someone to talk to? And he does have *some* good qualities.

Have I mentioned the sex?

Good night, Dearest Diary.

From 'PTSD Nation – The New 'ism for a New Generation' (pp. 14-15) by Jerry Barnes, Ph.D., Ed.D., former M.D.

"So you ask, Good Reader, how can you as an individual support the troops?

Kind words, such as, 'thank you for your service,' go a long way. Nothing more need be said and it is often best that nothing more *is* said.

This issue is especially sensitive with family. Often, and with all good intentions, a parent, a sibling, an aunt or uncle etc. will ask about the service member's experiences in war. This is most often a no-no. If the veteran wants to talk about their experiences they will. If they don't, there is often good reason for it.

If your vet at some time becomes willing to discuss their wartime service, even *then* it is best to listen, not talk. And whatever you do, *do not* tell the vet that his or her actions were incorrect, stupid, wrong, or made no sense. Remember, Good Reader, war does not make sense. Don't think for any minute that any part of it does. Human beings are not programmed, by nature, to take another human being's life.

And *do not*, under any circumstances, ask the most painful question for so many veterans struggling with unwanted memories; 'Did you kill anybody?'

Now, this would seem like common sense to most of you, but in my more than eight decades on planet earth, I have discovered that common sense just isn't so common. So, in light of this lack of common sense, let's call it respect. Have enough respect for your vet, or any vet, not to ask this.

If you were to have done that which is considered amongst almost all societies and religions on earth, the most heinous thing that could be done, take another's life, would you want to be reminded of it?

Would you ask a rape victim to rehash her time of terror? You think I am stretching scenarios here? Just as alcoholism does not discriminate between the guy living on Park Avenue, drinking 100 year old wine in his penthouse to excess, and the guy living on the park bench with his Mad Dog 20/20, Post Traumatic Stress Disorder does not discriminate between those whom it afflicts, be they rape victims, accident survivors or veterans.

Engage your brain before opening your mouth. It's a pretty good policy.

4

Who is this? Corey thought, looking at the unknown number on his cell. *Someone else wanting money I don't have for some dumb shit that bitch did while I was gone?*

"Hello?"

"Corey!"

"Jennifer?"

"Yeah, hey. It's me."

"Something wrong?"

"Well, I have something coming up on the date of our next appointment, and I was wondering if we could reschedule?"

"Sure," he said. "You know I don't have anything going on. You guys must be busy there. I would imagine your assistant would call from the VA number for any rescheduling. I didn't recognize your number and almost didn't answer."

"Oh yeah," she said, though '*Oh shit*!' is what she thought. "We've been swamped, but can you come in Friday? 3:00 p.m.?"

"Let me check my schedule," he said. She relaxed and smiled on the other end of the line. "Nope. Nothing going on. Sure, I'll be there."

"Great!" she said, the sudden rush of relief in her voice obvious. "I'll go ahead and change the van pick up for you. You still need the van, right?"

"Oh yes," he said. "Still don't have a license. But I'll get there."

"I know you will, Corey. See you Friday."

"See you then."

From '<u>PTSD Nation – The New 'ism for a New Generation</u>' (pp. 18-19) by Jerry Barnes, Ph.D., Ed.D., former M.D.

"And now, Good Reader, we come to the section on drugs. Rather, one of many sections on drugs, for these magical entities are being used in full force both on the battle field during deployment and here at home upon the service member's return.

Let's look at the first group, one that is arguably necessary in theater to allow our troops to 'continue the mission.'

The sleeping pills!

One can imagine that in an environment of high stress, both physical and psychological, one may have trouble sleeping. Add together the already irregular sleep hours and patterns, constant explosions and irregular schedules, and Viola! Sleeping pills!

What pills and in what amounts are being used? How many soldiers are taking them?

Believe it or not, as of the writing of this manuscript, it turns out that the data needed to reach any solid conclusions about actual, clear use of pharmaceuticals among the ranks of our military isn't available. The military doesn't keep tabs on the drugs its troops take, though it is estimated that the number of active military personnel (this does not even include guard and reserve members on active orders also taking drugs) has surpassed 100,000.

Now, is the lack of record keeping a simple oversight? Or is there something more ominous at work behind the reasons as to why these records are not kept?

One sleeping agent that we know is being used in full force, as reported directly from returning troops themselves, is a drug called Klonopin. Klonopin is a very effective, yet highly hallucinogenic drug that gives the user the sleep they need, but one hell of a hangover and some 'far out and groovy trips, man' when they come off of the drug.

Soldiers in both theaters in the Middle East have reported waking up at times, not knowing exactly where on God's green earth they are, and why it is they are there. Fear not for their safety too much, Good Reader, for although they are oblivious to their surroundings, they are heavily armed with enough fire power to take out any threat, be it real or perceived, civilian or military, in sight.

Now, of course I say this tongue in cheek, but alas, it is a cold hard fact that these young men and women are waking up in states in which they would certainly serve jail time back here at home if they were ever to operate a motor vehicle on the public roads *in* such state.

But not to worry, Good Reader, because they aren't here driving those little Japanese imports that might weigh as much as a standard refrigerator.

They are far, far away, driving 70,000 pound up-armored gun trucks with enough munitions inside to take out a city.

*

*Meeting between Jennifer Hutton (L.C.S.W.) and Corey Prine
- October 19, 2009

"I'm glad I was able to get you in today, Corey."

"Hey," he said, spreading his arms wide. "You know how busy
I am." He chuckled lightly, bringing his arms in and then
crossing his hands on his lap.

"You seem relaxed today," Jennifer said.

"More so than you," he said, never blinking and maintaining
eye contact.

"Corey, I'm going to be honest with you about something."

"Ok." Still not blinking.

"I don't have anything going on when we were originally
scheduled to meet."

"I know," he said.

"How do you know?"

"Because your office would have called. You wouldn't have used your cell phone.I worked for the government, too, remember?"

"Let's go back to square one, Corey. I mean, we need to start over with something very important."

"Sure."

"Last time you were here, after you left I mean, I went back over your pre-admin questionnaire because we'd talked about drug and alcohol use. I wanted to make sure you were still answering 'no' on the forms because you told me you hadn't been drinking or using."

"Didn't trust me, huh?"

"Oh no, Corey! It isn't that. I trust you. You are so open and I believe everything you tell me. You really are one of my favorites.

"But technically, I am supposed to go over those forms at every appointment. I don't always do it. Not with vets like you who I know are being honest and open with me. But when I did, I noticed something disturbing that hasn't been discussed between us."

"What's that?" he asked, a look of concern on his face.

"When you've been asked if you felt like hurting yourself or others, you've been saying 'yes.' Even after the sessions we've had, and you seem to be doing better, you're still answering 'yes.' Why have you not mentioned anything about this to me?"

"You haven't asked," he said. "And I just figured you wouldn't care to talk about it anyway."

"I *haven't* asked, Corey, and I'm sorry, but why would you think I wouldn't be concerned? Of course I'm concerned. That's why I called you back in early."

"The ass clown at demobe didn't seem to care, so I just thought you wouldn't either."

"What are you talking about?"

"When we were at demobe, we had to do these exit interviews with a shrink after turning our gear in and going to the dentist and all that crap. I guess they needed to make sure we were safe to turn loose on society." He paused, looking down and to the left, recalling the memory.

"Anyway," he continued. "This guy asked me if I felt like hurting myself or others. I told him 'of course I do!' I mean, I'd just come back from hell. I was treated like a fucking prisoner in an institution by my leadership. My ex wife had reamed out my bank account while I was gone. With the help of her new faggot boyfriend. They wrecked my fucking truck and sold it for parts and partied with the insurance money! And then they took my son (*one year, nine months and fifteen days old now*) and ran off somewhere. Of course I wanted to hurt myself or… no. AND someone else!"

His face was red and his brow was covered with sweat. He was sitting forward now and his eyes had taken on a crazed look.

"Corey," she said, putting a hand out. "Sit back, take a deep breath and relax. You're here with me, and I care. I'll listen. Just catch yourself and tell me how that went with the guy at demobe."

He did as she said, except for taking a deep breath. He needed to take three before he could continue. One Mississippi… Two Mississippi… Three Mississippi…

"He told me that whatever I do, *not* to tell that to anyone there."

"What?" Now Jennifer was sitting forward in her seat, and her eyes were bulging. "He said what?"

"Yeah," he said. "He told me that if I said yes to that question that they'd lock me up. Put me on some psych ward or something for six months and that I'd *never* get to go home. It put the fear of God in me. I mean, I'd been gone for a year, and even though I wasn't coming back to the life I had before, I *was* coming back. All I wanted to do was get away from the Army, sleep in late, take my time eating a meal. Go for a few days without shaving.

"So he asked me again, I guess after he gave it all time to sink in, if I wanted to hurt myself or others. So I told him no."

"Wow!" Jennifer said, sitting back and breathing deeply herself now. One Mississippi…

It wasn't the first time she'd had a vet relay this information to her from the demobe sites scattered across the country. But it *had* been a while since she'd heard it. More than a year. She'd hoped with all the wreckage so many of the returning troops had caused; murder, suicide, etc. that they had put an end to this incompetence at the demobe sites, but obviously not.

"Corey," she finally spoke. "I care. I honestly do. Do you know that?"

"I do," he said. He could tell Jennifer was genuine. He'd been able to tell that from their first meeting. "It's why I've shared as much with you as I have, Jennifer. From the first session. For some reason I feel safe showing you things I'd never show anyone else."

"You don't know how much I appreciate that, Corey," she said. "Now, can I prove this to you even more by having your permission to get into some of the areas we haven't talked about? Your marriage, your finances, those things?"

"If you'd like," he said.

"Do you feel like these are the things that make you feel like hurting yourself or others? I mean, who do you want to hurt? Yourself or someone else?"

"Both," he said.

"Why do you feel like hurting yourself? Is it because you get so depressed? You feel like life just isn't worth living anymore because of what's happened?"

As she spoke, she was typing frantically, pulling up the VA's protocol for this situation, though she already knew what it was.

Meds.

"Not really," he said.

She stopped typing. She had expected a 'yes,' or at least a 'kinda,' but not a 'not really.'

"What do you mean, 'not really?'" she said, and then she turned to face him.

"I feel at times like maybe I should kill myself so I don't kill someone else."

"Like your ex-wife?"

"Not really."

Oh shit Jen, another 'not really.' And his eyes. They look like they did before. His eyes!

"Then who, Corey?"

"Sometimes, anybody."

"What do you mean by that, Corey? Do you have rages? Get angry all of a sudden and feel like hurting whoever just happens to be around you?"

"Look Jennifer," he said, leaning forward and lowering the tone of his voice. "I appreciate the relationship we have, the trust, the honesty, and the fact that you care. I'm not going to sit here and waste your time. I'm going to tell you like it is. Like it *really* is."

"Okay," she said, sitting back and crossing her arms, her protocol search finished but forgotten. "Tell me like it really is."

"You remember when I told you that I was a trained killer? And that I went to Iraq not to kill, but to be a water boy?"

"Yes." Her kid caught in the cookie jar 'yes.'

"Well, ya see, the U.S. Government, through their armed forces, has perfected the art of creating killers. Like I mentioned before, they train us to kill, desensitize us from killing and then motive us to kill."

"Yes, they've perfected that," she said.

"Well, something they haven't perfected and haven't even cared to address is how to *re-sensitize us*. How to *turn it off,* so to say, once we come home."

This guy is a fucking genius, Jennifer thought as she sat listening.*Oh, how many beers my colleagues and I have drunk while having this very conversation!*

"The thoughts are always there," he continued. "The drive and motivation is there, and when you go to do it and aren't allowed to do it, a sort of morbid curiosity comes along later to join the thoughts and the drive and motivation. What would it have been like? What *would* it be like?

"It never goes away.

"There is no off switch!"

Oh shit, Jen!

She glanced at the computer screen. *Yep!* Just as she'd suspected. VA protocol for suicidal/homicidal thoughts?

Meds!

Pill of choice?

Citalopram.

"Thank you for sharing this with me, Corey." She sat up in her chair, looking down from the screen to the top of her desk, collecting her thoughts. What to say next?

"Is this normal?" Corey asked before she could say anything.

"It is Corey. But most vets, the ones I work with at least, aren't vocal about it. Some of them simply don't know how to express these emotions in words. You really made it crystal clear."

"So where do we go from here?"

"My computer here," she said, pointing at her screen while sitting back in her chair again, "says to prescribe you Citalopram."

"But I thought you weren't a fan of meds?" His face looked as confused as his voice sounded.

"I'm not," she said. "In almost all cases. But in this case, I think we should follow the proto-… (she caught herself) the recommendation. It's just a small, beginner dosage of 10 milligrams. It takes up to ten days to get into your system. I'd like to get you started on this, just as a precaution, and have you back in two weeks."

He was looking at her like he'd been betrayed. Like she was no better than the ass clown at the demobe station.

"Corey." She could read his thoughts by the look on his face. "Trust me on this one. It isn't enough of a dosage to make enough of a difference for you to notice it consciously. It may actually help you sleep better at night. Have you still been having trouble sleeping?"

"Oh, yeah," he said, his look of mistrust softening but not disappearing. "Still can't sleep."

"Okay," she said. "This is just enough to get you to sleep. But the real healing is going to come from our discussions. I want you back in two weeks, and I want you to be prepared to address some of the stuff you haven't opened up with me about yet. Your ex-wife. Your leadership.

"You've alluded to some abuse by your leadership a couple of times now. I want to hear about that. And you *have* to get it out Corey, or you'll never get past it. Can you do all this?"

"Yeah," he said.

"Great," she said. "As I've said, I can't prescribe. I have to go down the hall to get you the script. Better yet, I'll just have our Doc intranet it over to the pharmacy. You know where that is, up at the main building?"

"Oh yeah," he said. The psychological treatment center sat over the hill from the main hospital, but Corey always had to go to the main building to check in for his appointments. He had been screened for hearing loss and other service connected injuries there as well. He knew the building, and he'd always passed the pharmacy and the endless sea of humanity lined up in front of the windows. "I know where it's at."

"There's usually a wait," she said. *More like a time out from the rotation of the earth on its axis is more like it*, she thought. "By the time you make it to the window it will be ready. Remember, 10 mg a night before bed. No more, no less. That's just one tiny pill. And we'll meet back here in two weeks. Same time, same place."

She had blocked the appointment into her computer while she spoke. She printed off the appointment slip and handed it to him. "See ya then, Corey."

"Bye, Jennifer."

    * Personal diary entry of Jennifer Hutton - October 19, 2009

    Dearest Diary,

I have good news and bad news for you today. The good news is that I covered my ass with Corey Prine! I was able to get him back in and finally address the homicidal/suicidal issues he faces, and put it in that damn computer at work that I have been dealing with this issue! Damn big brother and his prying eyes! But hey, the notes are there now and I'm covered, but I still pray nothing happens.

More good news. Corey has agreed to start talking about some of the serious issues we haven't discussed yet, but I don't think this is where the dangerous tendencies or thoughts he's been having is coming from. I can understand more now why he made me nervous on our first meeting. The guy is like a fox in a hen house as the locals would say. He just hasn't been in any hen houses yet and to my knowledge hasn't been looking for any. But he is definitely a fox. He is super intelligent. He has great personal insight and can read people, at least me, like a book.

Ok, bad news. I did it again. I prescribed more meds, this time to Corey. Citalopram.

Ok, so I didn't prescribe it because I can't. But I had the button pushing monkey down the hall prescribe it. God, every time I go in there, whether Jack is working or Regina, all I do is say the vet's name and the drug and then they look at me like I'm wasting their time, type it in and send it over to the pharmacy. Just like that, no questions asked.

But at least it is only 10 mg. I'm covering my ass again. Following protocol.

God, I feel a visit to Dr. Barnes is long overdue. I wonder if he's even still alive. Jesus, he must be a thousand years old by now.

Oh, of course he's alive! When that man dies, the world will mourn. Well, in private of course. No one in my practice would get caught mourning him publicly.

That's it, Dearest Diary, my mind is made up. I'm driving out to see those old bones called Dr. Barnes this weekend!

Oh, Rob called, but I'm not up for him. Not tonight.

And I *did* go to the gym. At my age, to have cheated the old cottage cheese thighs is no accident. It comes from work baby! Lots and lots of work! And this evening's work? One hour lifecycle and then a dip in the hot tub.

Good night, Dearest Diary.

*

From 'PTSD Nation – The New 'ism for a New Generation'
(pp. 20-21) by Jerry Barnes, Ph.D., Ed.D., former M.D.

"And what, you might ask, are our service men and women given upon their return in the way of medications? Well, certainly more Klonopin if they request it. It is often recommended. But so many troops report having had so many bad experiences with the drug, or rather, from coming off the drug that they defer. This leads us to the 'next best thing' as deemed by the VA (no doubt due to a large contract with a pharmaceutical company), Citalopram.

Citalopram is an SSSI, which stands for selective serotonin re-uptake inhibitors, or serotonin-specific re-uptake inhibitor. SSRIs are a class of compounds typically used as antidepressants in the treatment of depression, anxiety disorders, and some personality disorders. It is the VA's first line of defense for PTSD or PTSD symptoms. Remember, as discussed in our opening section of this great work of literature I am undertaking, the difference between PTSD and PTSD type symptoms boils down to one thing; money.

If a vet is approved for suffering from what is sure to become known in the future as the great 'ism of the first half of the twenty first century, he or she gets paid. If not, they are still treated for the symptoms, but they receive no disability payment and they must pay for their own medications.

And what happens if they can't afford to pay? Well, they can always simply go without.

Now, please note some of the adverse side effects associated with Citalopram. These include apathy, headaches, tinnitus, fatigue, insomnia, weight loss, loss of sexual drive, mania, tremors and dissociative and cognitive disorders (loss of contact with reality).

What? You ask. Aren't these the very symptoms of PTSD from which the afflicted suffers?

Bingo, Good Reader! You have won the grand prize! Now, what was I saying about that large contract between the VA and some large pharmaceutical company?

5

*Meeting between Jennifer Hutton (L.C.S.W.) and Jerry
Barnes, Ph.D., Ed.D., former M.D. October 21, 2009

"This way please," the petite, Asian nurse's assistant,
Mina, said to Jennifer before leading her through the house.

The house of Jerry Barnes, the swami- the guru- the man
whose books and essays are kept and constantly referenced by
everyone in the mental healthcare field (in secret of course)
but whose name is never to be spoken.

Jerry Barnes- the outlaw- the banished, excommunicated from
his profession like Copernicus had been from the Catholic Church
all those years ago for daring to state and teach that the earth
and all of the other planets in our solar system revolve around
the sun and not visa/versa.

It only took the Church 400 years to pardon Copernicus. Perhaps, in equal time, Dr. Barnes would be forgiven and pardoned within his field.

Mina led Jennifer to Dr. Barnes' private study in the back of the house. From the door, Jennifer looked through a wall sized bay window on the far side of the room and out into the yard where another young lady- not Asian, but still petite and very pretty, and whose name was Anna, was raking leaves freshly fallen from a giant poplar tree. In front of the window sat a frail, old man in a wheelchair.

This was Dr. Jerry Barnes.

"So, the prodigal student returns," he said, peering at her reflection in the window. "To what do I owe the honor?" He turned in his wheelchair to face her. He had a thin oxygen tube in his nose, the line running down and hooking to a small tank on the frame of the wheelchair, and he had an afghan on his lap. "That will be all, Mina."

The man could pass for Carl Sagan's long lost twin brother. He had a small head that looked larger than it really was on his small, rickety frame. His beady little eyes looked even beadier behind his pop bottle thick glasses, as if one were looking at them through a pair of binoculars held backward. And where Sagan had been intellectually blessed in the physical sciences, Barnes had been equally blessed in the behavioral sciences.

Barnes was to Pavlov what Sagan was to Einstein. A little bit, or a lot of Freud came out in his personal perversions.

"She's cute," Jennifer said, nodding after Mina, who was making her way down the hall. Then she walked into the room and sat down in an overstuffed leather chair on one side of a small fire place.

"Yes," he said, watching Mina go. "She's from the Philippine Islands, here on a working visa. The poor thing, she works so hard, but all of her money goes to her family back in the islands and I fear they are not being responsible with it. I've tried to convince her to save some of it for herself, but alas, it's hard to overcome ingrained culture.

"I've always enjoyed surrounding myself with beautiful women, Jennifer," he said, now turning his full attention to her. "That was one of the reasons I always enjoyed you so much."

"It's been a while," she said, ignoring the flattery. *Dirty old man*, she thought, *still the same*. "I just wanted to come out and see how you were doing."

"I'm eighty five years old now, Jennifer," he said, adjusting the tube in his nose and then repositioning the afghan on his lap. "My doctors told me I'd be dead from this goddamn lung disease in three months. That was in 1975. I didn't have time for bullshit then and I don't have time for it now. Shall we dance?" A smirk graced his face. Straight to the point, please.

"I think I have a problem patient."

"Of course you do, dear. That's why you're here. Now, come then. What's the problem?"

"He's homicidal and suicidal."

"Oh yes, aren't they all that way?" He glanced down at his lap, his hands buried under the afghan. "I'd hoped the almighty U.S. Government would have let me die in peace. No more wars until I was gone. No chance of that it seems. Too many starving S.U.V.'s on our streets and too much oil in the Middle East." He paused, smiling now and shaking his head.

"You watch," he continued. "We'll be fighting all tropical nations in fifty years for bananas and mangos. Oh, yes," he said, sensing her smirk. "A great food shortage is in this world's future and you'd better believe the guys with the guns and the bombs will be the ones getting what's left. The illustrious C.I.A. is off installing puppet governments all along the equator as we speak, getting ready."

"Dr. Barnes," she said, not a bit interested in his futuristic predictions or conspiracy theories. "I'm afraid this guy might do something. I mean, he's smart. He's really smart. I'm afraid he's the one that might get pushed the wrong way and just go off."

She settled more into the chair, paused and breathed. One Mississippi…. "I think he's the type that could do a lot of damage and never get caught."

"You haven't put any of this in your notes at work have you? In your computer?" He looked at her with a look that was as serious as a heart attack. He had placed one hand over his chest while speaking as if he were having one.

"Oh hell no!" she said. "Of all the things I've ever learned from you, that lesson has stuck the most. I keep these concerns in a personal handwritten diary at home."

'Never put anything that can come back and bite you in the ass in professional notes,' he had told her years ago.

The two had been introduced by a mutual friend, Byron Blevins, a former student of Dr. Barnes' working with Jennifer at the VA in Beckley after having pulled a short stint as a social worker with Nicholas County in Summersville. The same Byron Blevins who had since been transferred to the VA in Salem, Virginia. Neither Dr. Barnes nor Jennifer missed him.

'Things are not like they were back in the good old days,' Dr. Barnes had said back then at one of their first meetings, 'when a counselor could openly and honestly try to help their patients to the best of their ability. Back before the *fucking lawyers* took over and ruined the field.'

In those days, 'fucking lawyers' had been one of his catch phrases. He used it less often now, but it was always in his hip pocket, ready for the quick draw.

'Only when our government was governed by three branches could we focus on doing the right thing' he'd bemoaned. 'But now that the legislative and executive branches have fallen asleep at the wheel, and we are governed only by the judicial, we must focus more on doing the *smart* thing.'

Jerry Barnes had practiced and taught psychology for half a century before losing his privileges to do both. On top of teaching, counseling, and writing, he had started volunteering his services in the late 1990's after his wife passed and he had found too much time alone on his hands. He was seeing patients

on the weekends on the behalf of the social security
administration; real down and outers.

He had been working with a man that had been in and out of
the system's revolving doors since returning from Vietnam in the
early 1970's. By the time Dr. Barnes got his case the man had
been homeless for years. He was an active alcoholic and drug
addict, in and out of jails and prisons and lunatic asylums,
barely alive.

The man was also suicidal. So much so that in the winter
during which Dr. Barnes had started seeing him, he found fit to
jump off of the New River Gorge, the longest arched bridge in
the western hemisphere and at one time, the world (damn Chinese,
the locals lamented). The New River below, 847 feet below, had
been frozen with ice nearly two feet thick, and his head had
smashed open like a jack-o-lantern that had been pushed off the
side of a porch rail a week after Halloween.

A porch rail from the top of a New York City high rise.

A miracle followed the man's suicide. His son, the one no
one seeking help for the old man had ever been able to find,
emerged.

And he emerged with a team of lawyers and a wrongful death
suit.

Dr. Barnes wasn't too surprised. The U.S., in his opinion,
had been getting more and more litigious through the last decade
of the twentieth century, and he knew that his home state, West
Virginia, was leading the nation in junk lawsuits per capita
(yes Badelia, there is a reason businesses won't set up shop in
the mountain state. And it isn't all because of the unions).

The social security department wasn't going to take any
heat. They deferred all blame to Dr. Barnes and then seized all
of his notes and voluntarily offered them up to opposing counsel
before they were even subpoenaed.

'You should have prevented this tragedy, Dr. Barnes,' the
mediator (a retired judge) had said during mediation. Mediation
was a newer technique at the time, an attempt to stem the

frivolous litigation sweeping America, or at least make the process move along quicker.

All these years later, Dr. Barnes would opine that mediation had turned into nothing more than the act of one willingly giving opposing lawyers and those they represented what they wanted without the generally accompanying public entertainment (trial) being involved. At the end of the day, the lawyers could handle more cases, which equaled more money for them; a more effective way of doing business.

Lady Justice and her scales! Weighing time against money, because time is money, Dr. Barnes thought. *And justice? You gotta pay for it! And man will it cost you!*

At the end of mediation, Dr. Barnes had given up his right to practice, his right to teach, and his right to continue counting the cold one million dollars paid out for suffering to the son of the deceased as part of his overall net worth.

This, or face criminal charges and jail time for manslaughter.

And everyone involved knew jail time for Dr. Barnes did nothing to help increase the lifestyle of poor 'ol junior, grieving son of the deceased. Only money could soothe his wounds and heal his aching heart. At least for eighteen months, the average amount of time in America that law suit awards, lottery winnings and inheritances last. A year and a half and it would all be gone. And Dr. Barnes knew this. Simple math about money; if you don't earn it, you don't keep it.

But Dr. Barnes still retained his right to write and publish, and being that he was one of the original God Fathers of current mental healthcare in the U.S., working with returning Vietnam vets, and then later rape and accident victims in regard to the concept of treatment for anxiety associated with having experienced traumatic events, before the 'ism as he called it, of Post Traumatic Stress Disorder had become a household name, anything appearing in print with his name on the byline sold, and it sold well.

He'd made his mediation loss back tenfold with the advent of the wars in the Middle East. A bitter sweet gain as he

certainly didn't enjoy profiting from them. But the wars had
allowed him to keep on keepin' on none the same. And everyone
who knew him, out of respect and in spite of the loss of his
medical license, still called him "Dr. Barnes."

*

"Even keeping such notes in a personal diary at home is
dangerous, love. The Gestapo can take what they want *when* they
want. Especially with this Patriot Act nonsense," Dr. Barnes
said.

"I'm just trying to keep it straight somewhere," she said.
"So I'll know what to do."

"If you knew what to do, you wouldn't be here, dear."

"Exactly!" she said.

Dr. Barnes turned his wheelchair and rolled to the large
bay window. Mina had joined her colleague, so now he had two
beautiful ladies to watch do yard work, one of his favorite
pastimes. "What does your protocol say to do?"

"It's cookie-cutter," she said. "Handed down from the hands
of the VA Gods. Citalopram."

"And?" he asked, his eyes still focusing on the girls in
the yard.

"And I prescribed Citalopram. Starting dose of 10 mg."

"And you are here because you know it won't help your vet
and may make him worse," he said, now turning back to face her.

"Partly," she said. "I was covering my ass by prescribing
it to him, and buying time to come see you."

"Why are you so concerned about this vet more than others
you work with, Jennifer?" His brain was fully engaged now, as if
he had had to take one last peep at his lady helpers to shut

them out of his dirty old man mind so he could focus exclusively on Jennifer's needs.

"He's psychotic!" she said.

He threw his head back in maniacal laughter. "Of course he's psychotic! They all are! They send these kids over to do what they do in these shit holes they have to do it in, and then they expect them to come back and fit into society as if they hadn't missed a beat.

"After seeing what they've seen? After doing what they've done? With most of the people around them once they return discrediting it all or simply not giving a damn either way? Of course he's psychotic, Jen."

"But there's something dangerous about this guy, Dr. Barnes," she said. "I can feel it. He hasn't done anything that I'm aware of, but he's so intelligent. He knows he's been turned into a killer. And he isn't buying the standard, 'It's your job as a returning vet to deal with your own 'isms'' line the D.O.D. feeds these guys at the demobe sites. He knows there is no re-sensitization. No 'off switch' as he called it himself."

"So you think that if this guy doesn't see the point of it all," he said, waving an all encompassing arm, "that he might just off himself, or perhaps a dozen others?"

"Yes," she said. "This guy could be the next Ted Bundy if he wanted to be. Or that copycat killer from out where I'm from, Ted Grundy."

Dr. Barnes winced at the thought, having seen the news report the night before on this Grundy guy out on the west coast, just south of Seattle. Grundy, the report had said, was awaiting indictment on what authorities were estimating could be more than one hundred killings in the now infamous, "Serial Street murders."

"I'm not so much concerned that he's suicidal as much as I am that he is homicidal," Jennifer continued. "And he is so smart; he could leave a trail of bodies between here and fifty years from now and never get caught."

A long silence passed before either of them spoke again, and when words were spoken again, it was Jennifer who spoke them. She said, "What do I do?"

"Monitor the Citalopram," he said. "I'm glad you prescribed it."

"What?" she asked, surprised. She knew Dr. Barnes cared for meds even less than she did.

"How old are you, dear? Thirty?"

"Yeah right," she said, laughing. "Close to forty."

"Too young regardless. Yes, too young to be pushed out of the industry. It isn't just a job for you, dear. You give a damn about the people you're trying to help. If you didn't give a damn, you wouldn't have come today. There is a doctorate in your future."

Jennifer looked down, confused. She had not gotten the answers she'd hoped to get by coming.

"Cheer up, dear," he said, as if reading her mind. "Get him talking as much as you can. About anything and everything. Keep me abreast as things progress. We'll dance again."

6

"I need a job," Corey said, clicking the pad on his laptop.

It was 2 a.m., and he still couldn't sleep. The Citalopram had taken some of the edge off, but his back still throbbed, his ears still rang. Even more it seemed since starting the meds.

And he was still pissed.

Speaking of pissed, half a dozen soda bottles filled with piss lined the wall beside his bed. Just another part of the deployment he couldn't seem to put behind him.

The piss bottles; always readily available in the gun truck while on mission, and in the CHU in case you woke up and had to go. With sleep as little and precious as it was, no one wanted to waste three minutes of precious time walking to the latrine, some forty meters away, piss, and then walk back. Get your heart rate up and make it harder to get back to sleep or run into some fobbit asshole like LT Bee and be forced to do some bullshit duty (needless task) and not get back to sleep at all.

Fobbits were soldiers who deployed to war but never left the F.O.B.- Forward Operating Base- also known as the 'Green Zone.' Only 7% of soldiers who deploy actually *do* leave the F.O.B., the other 93% never do, this being a little known fact not only among civilians, but also among many within the military.

Like another little known fact about deployments; the same forty percent of military personnel keep deploying over and over and over, while the other sixty percent never deploy at all due to rank, job description, or friends in high places. Oh, the things your recruiter *doesn't* tell you.

Those recruiters, who don't deploy either.

But fobbits weren't bad people; they just weren't part of the combat arms M.O.S's that left the wire. They did their specific jobs and most of them did them well, and their lives were in every bit as much danger as the combat arms guys, at least in Mosul. The F.O.B. was mortared every day and every night, so even the supply assistants and paper pushers at the T.O.C. (Tactical Operations Center) could be killed at any given time.

The only problem any of the soldiers who left the wire *really* had with the fobbits was that they were always buying up all the goods at the PX (post-exchange).

And speaking of mortar attacks, they had been almost non-stop while Corey and his unit were in Iraq. And no one wanted to be "that guy" they found dead with his dick in his hand and his pants around his ankles, blown fifty feet away, because the shitter got hit by a mortar. Piss bottles were safer.

Corey had damn near reached the end of the internet in the months since returning from Iraq. And he'd gotten bored with all of it; Youtube videos, free movie downloads, Googling the names of his friends and families (and being surprised by some of the information he found). He'd even gotten sick of porn. All the vaginas of the world now looked the same to him.

But now he found himself feeding darker perversions. Perversions he couldn't remember having before.

Before what?

The war? The military?

Bondage and torture porn had given way to darker scenes; murders, killings, black market snuff films.

What's on prime-time tonight, Corey thought, clicking away. *More beheadings from the Middle East? Radical Islamic law in action.*

How about the one where they bury that chick up to her armpits in Pakistan and stone her to death for adultery, he thought. *How dare the whore bitch go out with another man! Her husband, who had probably been the childhood best friend of one of her grandfathers, had only been dead for three years. Serves her right!*

"God I need a fucking job."

*

*Meeting between Jennifer Hutton (L.C.S.W.) and Corey Prine- November 5, 2009

"So how's everything, Corey?"

"Good," he said, smiling, even with his eyes this time.

"I can tell," she said. "You look more relaxed. Do you think the Citalopram is working?"

"I think so," he said. "I mean, I'm still having a hard time sleeping. But that might be because of my back and the ringing in my ears. I feel a little less stressed though."

"Good," she said, typing notes into her computer. "How long have you been back now? Six months or so?" She leaned back in her chair, her notes done.

"Something like that. Yeah, I've done three drills with my new unit, so I guess it's been about six months."

"You should be hearing about your VA disability decision soon then."

"Yeah," he said. "I stopped off and talked with Angie up there at claims after I checked in this morning. She said I'm in front of the line with the other vets from Iraq and Afghanistan, and that I should get the decision letter any day now."

"Don't set yourself up for disappointment," she said. "I'm sure you'll get something, for PTSD and the tinnitus if nothing else. Almost everyone is getting that. But they always give you a lower rating at first. Be prepared for half of what you are expecting and be prepared to file an appeals claim. They work like an insurance company, ya know. They hope nine out of ten people will accept their decision and go on with life and not question it, and about half of them will."

"I know," he said nonchalantly. "Angie's told me that every time we've talked. But hey, anything at first is better than nothing."

"I know, but just be ready." She paused, taking in his calm demeanor. She liked it but knew not to be fooled by it. Violent waters often ran beneath calm surfaces. "So how are we on other things?" she finally said. "Do you still feel like hurting yourself or others?"

"Sometimes," he said, grinning impishly and shrugging his shoulders.

"Same as before?"

"Yes."

"Ok," she said. "The meds can only go so far. We need to get it out Corey. Let's talk."

"Pick a topic," he said. "You're the boss."

"Have you had any contact with your ex-wife? Heard anything about your son?"

"No."

One year, nine months and four days old now, he thought. *God I miss you little buddy.* He looked to the floor, still relaxed, but his mood now somber.

God it's killing him, she thought. *His son. Later, Jen, later.*

"Let's talk more about Iraq," she said. "Is that ok?"

"Yeah," he said, monotone. "What do you want to know?"

"Well, you've mentioned abusive leadership a couple of times. Can you tell me about that a little?"

"Sure," he said, shaking off the previous thoughts of his son. "It all started at premobe really. Our leadership started becoming hard-asses.

"I could understand it at the time though. I mean, it was the National Guard, not the Army. Some of the privates drank beer on the weekends with the NCO's and officers. Some of them worked together. I used to go fishing with staff sergeant Reynolds."

"So you feel they were drawing the line between friendship and professionalism?"

"Sure," he said. "Some of the younger guys had a problem with it. Thought their buddies had turned into dicks. But I tried to explain it to them."

"You were a specialist, is that right?"

"Yeah, an E-4. Still a Joe, but not a private."

"So did this continue? Even in Iraq, once you mobed?"

"Not with most of the leadership, but there were a couple. Mostly this little half man with a major Napoleonic complex. Lieutenant Bee.

"We had a meeting when we first got there and he told us never to call him "LT," which is a common nickname for someone of his rank. He said he wasn't our buddy, he was our lieutenant, and he'd make sure we understood that. Told us all this shit about how he wished it was still 'old Army days' and not 'new Army days.'"

"What's that mean? Old Army, new Army?"

"Oh, it's generational envy crap," he said. "You know, like how your parents used to walk uphill both ways to school in three feet of snow on a ninety degree day? Killed black bears with their trapper keepers and shit?"

Jennifer laughed. "Sorry," she said. "That's funny. I get it."

"Yeah," he continued. "I guess in the old Army days, the days being before 9-11, if a soldier got out of line or if his leadership just didn't like him, they'd take him around the corner and slap him around a little… or a lot. Square him away as we call it. But after the wars started, they were forced by *their* chain of command to stop that. Big Army needs all the boots on the ground they can get. Don't need to scare people off with beat downs."

"So LT. Bee wanted to beat you guys, huh? Wanted you to know that he wanted to, and that he only didn't because he couldn't?"

"Sure," he said. "Hell, I wish he would have tried. He was maybe five feet five, and all of a hundred and fifty pounds. Squatty little fucker. Pissed off at the world about it, too."

"Sounds like classic Napoleonic complex," Jennifer said.

"Well, he was kinda smart though. He was a software programmer in the private sector. So he was still able to fuck with people he didn't like without making physical contact."

"How so?"

"He liked to fuck with our basic needs, like sleep and food."

"How did he do that?"

"Several ways. Like in premobe, if we had to do a night fire range, where we had to go to a range and practice shooting in the dark with night vision, an exercise that should have lasted maybe three hours, he'd make sure to sign enough rounds out from ammo to keep us there till sun-up. Then we'd have to train the whole next day as well. He'd keep us up till mid-night of that night, making us clean our weapons."

"Wow!" she said. "Two days without sleep?"

"Close to it," he said.

"That must have been equally hard on him though."

Corey threw his head back with laughter. "Yeah right. That little fucktard would go back to the bay and sleep all night every night and most of the afternoon, every afternoon."

"Wow! Quite the hypocrite, huh?"

"R.H.I.P. is the acronym he'd use. 'Rank Has Its Privileges.' But even with that I didn't mind so much. As we found out in-country there were plenty of times we went without sleep." He paused. "Not that even those times were necessary though." He spoke softer. "Come to think of it, yup! Those times were pretty much because LT Bee was fuckin' with us too."

"Even in theater?" she said, surprise in her voice.

"Oh yea," he said. "I mean, common sense would allow an earthworm to understand that when we were down, or not on mission, that we needed to rest up for the next one. We rolled every night, but LT Bee was a fobbit over there. The X.O."

He looked at her to make sure she understood both terms; fobbit and X.O., X.O. being the company officer next in line to replace the commanding officer. Her nod let him know that she understood the terms.

"He would bitch and complain that while we were 'out riding around in trucks all night' he and all the other fobbits were back there doing all the work. Can you believe that shit? Pure fuckin' penis envy!"

He paused again, catching his breath. Sweat beads swelling on his head.

"So anyway, when we were on the FOB, trying to sleep, that fucker would wake us up and make us go do stupid shit, like wash the gun trucks on the wash racks or go take stupid classes."

"Classes?"

"Oh yeah," he said. "Look, the way it worked out with our mission schedule, we were supposed to sleep from 6 a.m. to 3 p.m., and then get up and get ready to roll that night. He'd schedule a class almost every fucking day at 10 a.m."

"That is the exact mid-point of your sleep time," Jennifer said.

"Exactly! And you knew you had to go to the class, so the anxiety associated with knowing kept you from being able to go to sleep, and then when you got back, you were so pissed off because of the stupid shit the class was about that you couldn't get to sleep then either."

"What were the classes on?"

"Oh my God! The dumbest shit that had nothing to do with anything. He'd have someone come in from finance and talk about estate and tax planning. One time it was on energy efficiency. Whether it was better to turn your computer off while it wasn't in use or let it go to sleep."

"No way," she said, sounding like a valley girl twenty years her junior.

"Yes way," he said. "And then there were the ranges. I mean, every other week we'd have to stay awake all day, between missions, to go to some range. And on some of them we were firing weapons all day, like the MK-19 grenade launcher, that weren't even authorized for use in theater anymore, because of the collateral damage they caused. You know, part of that whole 'occupation' thing no one wanted to admit to?"

"I have never heard of anything this ridiculous, Corey."

"I know," he said. "I've talked to other vets from other wars or active Army guys about it and they think I'm making half this shit up. But I'm not. Those were his ways and his rules. He loved to make up his own rules to fuck with us.

"Hell, he got a rule passed in our company that if any maintenance was required on our vehicles that was not above any work explained in the dash-10, the little 'owner's manual' so to say that was inside the truck, that we had to do it after mission, not the mechanics. So we were now eighty eight mikes and sixty three bravos (MOS for light wheel mechanics). We had to stay up and do the work after rolling in from mission."

"What kind of work did this entail?"

"Oil changes, tire replacements, shit like that. And don't forget, the wheels on those gun trucks weigh more than a thousand pounds each."

"Did you have to do any of that work, Corey?"

"Yeah. We all did. Probably added to the back problems I have now."

"No doubt," she said.

"We had some pretty cool-ass mechanics though. They only let that shit go on for a few weeks. Then they told us, in secret, just to let them know what needed to be done and they'd do it when Half Man wasn't around. That's what we all called LT. Bee behind his back, Half Man."

"Sounds fitting," she said. "Wow. So he didn't think you guys were busy enough, so he gave you all that extra work."

"Yeah," he said.

"Was there nowhere you could go for help? Anyone to step in?"

"Oh, that's another story," he said. "There was. The Inspector General- or I.G. The I.G. guys are very high ranking officers whose sole goal in life is to find abusive leadership and weed them out.

"LT. Bee told us in that first meeting we had in Iraq, that no one was *ever* to go to I.G., and that if we did, and he found out about it, that he would make our lives a living hell. He said we would remember having narked him out for the rest of our lives."

"So, like an abusive parent, he scared you through intimidation. Like an abusive father might say, 'don't ever tell your mother, or I'll beat you even worse the next time she's not around,'" Jennifer said.

"Exactly, and then you come back and people think that if you didn't kill anyone or get your ass blown off by an I.E.D., you didn't do shit. I worked harder over there in the nine months we were actually in theater than I've ever worked in any five year period of my life back here. I feel like I aged at least ten years over there. And then to come home to a life resembling nothing of the one I left? Really? And I didn't do shit because I didn't kill anyone, or get blown up? That's the attitude?"

He was leaning forward in his chair now, his face red and sweaty. His eyes had taken on that same appearance that had made her so nervous in their first session.

Oh God, she thought. *There are those eyes again. And he's rubbing his hands on the chair arms like everyone else now. Shit Jen, reign this one in.*

"Calm down, Corey. You aren't there anymore."

He sat back, breathing deeply. He wiped the sweat from his face with the palm of his right hand and then wiped it onto his pants leg.

Thank God. Not the arm of the chair.

"Was there anything else this guy did?"

"Yeah," Corey said, collecting himself. "He fucked with our food. All the time."

"What do you mean he fu… Excuse me. Messed with your food?"

"It started at premobe too. If we were gonna be on the range all night, getting there before dinner, he'd tell the soldiers at the chow hall responsible for bringing out our field chow not to bring it. That we were training to fight. Going without food."

"Is that legal?" she asked. She found herself hating this Half Man she'd never met.

"No," he said. "But remember. R.H.I.P. Everyone was afraid to rat him out."

"Oh yes," she said. "The system."

"The system," he agreed. "Anyway, it was worse once we got to Iraq. We didn't need to get to the motor-pool at first until 7 p.m. We rolled out of the gate between ten and eleven at night. That gave us plenty of time to make sure the trucks were functional and to load the communications on the radios. That kinda stuff.

"Anyway, he started making us take out the radios, the weapons, the ammo, everything, after every mission. So every fuckin' day we'd have to sign all that shit out from supply. It was a pain in the ass for supply and a pain in the ass for us. He did it so we'd have to go to the motor-pool at 4 p.m. Dinner chow was from 5 p.m. to 7:30 p.m."

"So you missed chow."

"Yes, we all missed chow."

"What did you do about eating?"

"Well, most of the guys just bought food at the PX and took it to the motor-pool. I couldn't afford that so I either went hungry or bummed."

"You couldn't afford it because you had a wife and kid back home?"

"No," Corey said. Now *he* used the tone that generally accompanied catching a kid in the cookie jar. "There's more to it than that."

"What do you mean, Corey?"

"Somehow, between the premobe site and the time we hit Kuwait, where we spent a couple weeks to adjust to the climate, the pay department fucked up my pay. I wasn't getting paid when we got there so I had no money."

"For how long?" she asked. "I mean, couldn't you just go to the pay department's office over there?"

"Oh sure," he said. "If LT Bee wasn't in your chain of command. I went to my team leader at the time, Sgt. Emerson. Great guy. Young, but fuck was he a hell of a leader. Anyway, he took it up the chain and when it got to LT Bee, he came to me and said he'd fix it and that under no circumstances was I to go to the pay department, because I was an E-4. I told him that my rank had nothing to do with my wife and kid needing to eat and pay bills back home. Boy was that a mistake."

"And why do you feel that was a mistake?"

"Because that son of a bitch didn't do shit about my pay issue, other than make sure that I never did anything about it myself. I went for *four months* with no pay."

"Wow!" Jennifer said. A long silence filled the room.

"Things got real bad after that," Corey said, finally breaking the silence.

"What happened after that?" she spoke softly, trying to keep the wild beast inside of him under control.

"It was like LT Bee developed this total, prison like mentality. By the way, his favorite thing to do in his free time was to watch 'Prison fights' on dvd in his CHU. They were black market I think."

"What are Prison fights?"

"Some really sick shit. Videos of prisoners fighting, like UFC. But you can't submit or get knocked out. Even once you are knocked out your opponent can continue to beat the hell out of you. Sometimes the guys get killed, and LT Bee loved that shit.

"Anyway, the guy just tried to make everyone's life hell. I mean, it got bad for me back home too. Hell, I wasn't taking care of my wife and kid because the army wasn't paying me. Legally she had every reason to up and leave me and take the kid. I wasn't supporting them. I tried to explain to her, that LT Bee was being a dick, but she wouldn't believe it. She refused to believe that the US Government would deploy a man to the war in Iraq, and then not pay him for up to four months while he was there."

"It does sound unbelievable, Corey. I know you're telling me the truth, but it's a story that sounds so unbelievable. I mean, you guys are over there doing what you do, and you aren't getting paid? Unbelievable!"

"Yeah," Corey said. "So while I'm out there looking for bombs and snipers, I'm worried about whether or not my baby has milk and diapers. I knew in my gut my wife was fucking around on me with that faggot from the bank. She worked with him. And I didn't have a pot to piss in as far as being able to do anything about it, because of LT Bee."

"What about your team leader? Sergeant Emerson, you said his name was?"

Corey nodded.

"Was he able to help you? Go to someone else in your chain of command?"

"He was dead a month later," Corey said, voice stoic.

"Oh my God," she said. "What happened? Can you talk about it?"

"He killed himself. Got the 'Dear John' letter and that was it. Lost his marbles.

"He went to LT Bee to talk about it a few days later. Came back, and ten minutes later we heard the shot go off in his CHU.

"Sergeant Brown went in and came out throwing up all over himself, yelling for the medic. The medic came, went in, and then came out throwing up all over himself too. I never went in and saw it. Didn't want to. That kid was my friend. That Goddamn LT Bee! I should have shot that mother fucker in the face that day!"

Jennifer remained silent for a few seconds before speaking.

"Corey?"

"Yes?"

He's had that crazy look in his eyes since we started talking about this, Jen. Shit.

"Do you have thoughts of going after Half Man? Do you want to kill him?"

Corey looked up, meeting her eyes with his own. He could see the chill it gave her. "No."

"Why not? I mean, I think even *I* would have those thoughts if I were in your position."

"That would be too easy. All they'd have to do is get a roster of who was under his command. Sure, all of us hated him by the end, and they'd probably question everybody, but they'd trace it back to me in the end."

"So do you have other plans of getting even?"

"Yes," he said.

"And what are those plans?"

"Let him live."

Jennifer looked confused and then asked, "What do you mean?"

"His life is miserable. That's why *he* is miserable. I'm sure the hell of his life is worse than death. Besides, if I'm gonna snap someday, I'm not making it so easy for people to find out about it."

Oh my God. Here it is Jen. Here it is.

"And do you feel like you are going to snap someday?"

Corey chuckled. His eyes were locked in that Jack Nicholson from "The Shining" look (come out and take your medicine, Danny).

"Now that would be too easy for you, Jennifer."

"What do you mean?" She was genuinely scared shitless now and hoped it wasn't showing.

"You're the Doc. No, let me get it right," he said, leaning back, breathing deeply and appearing calm. Not the kind of calm that came with serenity and peace, but the kind that stemmed from a mad man with a master plan. "You are the licensed clinical social worker, though you'll be a Doc someday. I'll leave whether or not I'm going to snap up to you to figure out."

"I need you to help me here, Corey. What's going on in your head?"

"It's been an hour," he said. "I have to go."

And he got up and walked out of her office.

*

*Personal diary entry of Jennifer Hutton- November 5 2009

Dearest Diary,

Just when I think I'm figuring things out, I'm convinced I don't know my ass from that proverbial hole in the ground.

Met with Corey Prine again today. I thought I had been making so much progress. Sure, when we were sugar coating our conversations. But today we started talking about some stuff that had really pissed him off. Some asshole named Lieutenant Bee who sounds like a total dick. I think I would have shot the guy myself if I had been under his command. I even shared this with Corey, but it didn't seem to sooth him any. He just kept getting angrier the more he talked about this guy.

This isn't new. But what *is* new is seeing someone like Corey, who has seemed to make great progress, revert to a state that is actually worse than the one he was in when I started working with him.

And those eyes of his, when he was really angry, God, they are creepy- super creepy- but somehow familiar, like I know them, like I've seen them before.

He was so upset that he left without confirming our next session. He called back an hour later to apologize, and I told

him he had nothing to apologize for, which he didn't. God my
heart goes out to this guy.

Rob has left a thousand messages on my cell phone and
facebook. I've really tried to steer clear of him, Dearest
Diary. I Promise. But I feel like, after today, I need to talk
to someone. He isn't the best prospect, but God, I'm a thirty
eight year old single chick in the middle of the bible belt. It
isn't like I'm back home where I could just go bar hopping on
Capitol Hill and run into two dozen friends.

Ok Rob, ready, though I'm really not, here I come. Pick up
your cell.

Good night, Dearest Diary.

*

Down in Hinton, Corey was sitting in bed and was back in
his head.

What a day, he thought. *And I thought these sessions were
supposed to be making me feel better, not pissing me off!*

He sure hadn't felt better on the way home. He didn't even
remember the ride. He had ridden in the front seat, and that fat
ass, peace time, "cold warrior" that he called himself, was

sitting in the seat behind him, going on and on about how "we never knew when the nukes were coming! We could'a been obliterated any time! Hey, I may not have gone overseas but we always had that mess to worry about! Us cold warriors just don't get enough recognition!"

But at least 'the *fat bastard,*' as Corey always referred to him in his mind, was getting paid by the VA. He bragged all the time about his 100% disability approval, which enabled him to get SSI automatically. Over $3,000 a month, tax free, for hanging out in garrison (stateside military base) for 8 years (two four year enlistments) and worrying about the evil Kremlin pushing the button before our own Commander in Chief, and coming out on the losing end of M.A.D. (mutually assured destruction).

The man had usually given Corey relief, hope that he *too* would get VA approval for some of his injuries, but on the way home he hadn't thought about that. At least he didn't *think* he'd thought about that.

The whole trip had seemed like a blackout. Remembering and talking about Half Man, LT Bee, had brought back anger and rage like he hadn't felt since he had been in Iraq.

Now he sat in his bed, alone, listening to Ozzie sing about paranoia. Was that the next stop on this crazy train?

LT Bee- what a prick.

So many memories were flooding Corey's mind, like the forced PT (physical training, or physical torture, depending on your level of fitness) in Iraq. And it wasn't just the forced trips to the gym in what very little time they had free. Sure, they would have preferred sleep, or to have watched a movie on their laptops, but LT Bee had forced them to the gym, and what little time they thought they would have as their own, alas had not been theirs. It had been LT Bee's time.

But what *had been* ridiculous about PT in Iraq had been the PT tests they were forced, by Half Man, to take every two weeks. That's right. While in theater, between combat missions, they were forced to do pushups and sit ups (as many as possible in two minutes) and forced to run 2 miles, for time, afterward.

Anyone failing to meet the minimum standards required to pass
the test was to lose rank and pay.

The standards weren't high. Not back home in garrison, but
in Iraq? Where the soldiers were going for 30 hours without
sleep regularly and more than a day without food at times?
Physical fitness just wasn't quite the priority that it had been
in garrison. And the soldiers could only force their bodies to
do so much, go so far.

Tell that to LT Bee though. The little prick had expected
everyone to meet the same standards as they had back home in
garrison.

That poor bastard Richards, Corey thought, remembering one
of his battle buddies from Iraq.

Pete Richards was older, mid-thirties, and though a college
graduate and high school history teacher, had joined the
enlisted ranks. His patriotism had made him want to take part in
the war on terror, regardless of rank, and he saw no need for
artificial glory by getting as far ahead in the ever, on-going
dick measuring contest the military called rank.

'The Patriot' they had all called him. 'Get me to the front
as quick as you can,' he'd told them at the enlistment station.
And sure enough, they had.

As a lower enlisted man; an E-4, specialist.

LT Bee had taken an extra special hatred toward Richards
from the start. The man was always reading, usually US history,
and sharing all the interesting facts he learned from doing so
with anyone who would listen.

The younger men in the platoon sought him out for fatherly
advice regularly. They seemed to listen more to him, though he
was a 'lower ranking puke' like they were, than their superiors.

Half Man had wanted to have his cake and eat it too. He
wanted to make sure everyone understood he was not their friend,
yet was envious whenever any of his troops would seek others out
for counsel.

But Richards, in spite of his age, was a PT stud. He had run track in college (while most of his fellow lower enlisted men were still in diapers) and had stayed in shape through the years as he aged. He could do 100 pushups and sit-ups each in two minutes, and run two miles in under eleven minutes (though he'd done it in only 9 ½ minutes in high school, he liked to boast). He led the entire Battery in results every time they were given a PT test.

Enter LT Bee and his forced PT tests in Iraq. PT tests which were not mandatory by the leadership above LT Bee. A memorandum had actually been passed down from the Command Sergeant Major in charge of the FOB in Mosul, stating that such tests were not required of soldiers in theater, and that he'd prefer if soldiers be allowed to save their energies for the mission, but that he would not interfere in each individual unit's chain of command's decisions. It was a "read between the lines you fucking morons" letter. Everyone read between the lines except LT Bee.

So, when Richards, for the first time in his military career, scored less than the perfect 300 on his test (a 298-even superman was getting tired from the deployment) LT Bee blew his stack and reprimanded him with a 'counseling statement,' a little piece of paper that in essence said, "You've been bad and I caught you being bad." Counseling statements were about as worthless as toilet paper, after being used. But LT had made his point.

In protest, on the next test two weeks later, Richards did the bare minimum of each exercise to obtain the minimal passing score of 180. He had actually whistled the whole time while doing sit ups (42 of them) to show that he could do the minimum amount required without even breathing.

Then came the wrath of LT Bee.

Richards didn't get two hours of sleep straight for the rest of the deployment (except for the time he was gunning and fell asleep in the turret and didn't see the handmade grenade thrown at his truck that cost him and his driver their hearing in one ear and half of that in the other).

LT Bee was always forcing him to do some useless detail while back on the FOB, like sweeping the offices at the T.O.C. or picking up the trash around the base. The trash the contractors like Halliburton's spin-off, KBR Inc. paid peasants from third world nations $400 a month to pick up (while banking the other $99,600 a month the defense department gave them for each employee they hired and calling it a profit).

That or go to the gym, where he was NOT allowed to run. Weights only. LT Bee knew how much the man loved to run and how important it was for his mental state while in theater.

Richards, in time, lost his mind and became a recluse. If he wasn't on mission, keeping to himself and often seen mumbling in his turret, he was on the FOB being Half Man's little bitch when he couldn't hide from him.

With two months left in the deployment, Richards had gotten a hernia while doing sit ups on a PT test, the result of sheer, physical exhaustion. The unit's PT stud not only finally fell from his thrown, but also had his intestines poke through his abs (quite loudly and painfully when it happened) when he did.

And LT Bee *refused* to let him seek medical attention. He threatened disciplinary action for the act of malingering (faking an injury or illness to get out of work). Instead, Richards' work for the half man went on, as did the forced PT tests, hernia or not.

When the unit got home and went through demobe, the doctors caught the injury and Richards was sent to the medical hold-over site at Fort Lewis in Washington State. The last Corey had heard he had spent two months in the hospital while the doctors fought a staff-infection that had almost killed him before they could perform surgery, and then two more months recovering from hernia surgery, getting hooked on Vicodin and various other pain pills while there.

The Wounded Warrior's Project had helped him get a teaching job at some backwoods high school in Grays Harbor County, Washington when he had gotten out of the hospital, in the general area of the notorious "Serial Street murders," but it hadn't lasted.

Three months into his teaching stint, and after he'd been hooked on Army and VA drugs and had run out of both, he had been caught smoking marijuana with an underage female student.

He had offered to plead guilty to the crime and do the time, but the local ass-hat police officers, 'former military themselves' they'd boasted (and no doubt cold warriors and fobbits) had told him that if he didn't wear wires and do set up stings and busts, become a nark in other words, that they would charge him with child molestation.

'We all know that little slut,' they'd told him in the privacy of their little offices. 'She's awfully damn cute and she's probably fucked the whole football team. And we think you fucked her! Come on, we would have. Now you help us out and we'll help you out. Give ya probation for six months and a $100 fine for contributing to a minor. Otherwise you're goin' away for twenty years!'

After LT Bee, Richards was *not* going to be another US Government agency's little bitch. And he wasn't going to be big Bubba's little bitch in some up state prison for something he hadn't done.

The last time he was seen, by a security camera at L.A.X. two days before a warrant had finally come out on his behalf for 'contributing to a minor'- a charge carrying up to 6 months probation and up to $100 in fines, he was on his way to some secluded, third world island nation in the South Pacific.

The patriot had expatriated.

And whatever became of LT Bee? After more than a dozen soldiers filed I.G. complaints upon returning from Iraq, the good 'ol boys system in the National Guard found fit to promote him to Captain (which came with a pay raise) and made him the C.O. of another battery within the unit.

"I'm gonna show all you mother fuckers!" Corey said, Ozzie Osbourne continuing to blare. "You want to treat us like felons in a penitentiary for raising our hands at a time of war and saying, 'Take me?' Well FUCK YOU!"

The scream was so loud that his parents would have heard it if they had still been awake. It actually caused his father down in the house below to roll from his left side to his right, and swat at his ear as if he'd been buzzed by a late season gnat.

"I'll get you, you fucks! I'll do exactly what you want me to do! What you've trained me to do! I'll be who you've made me be!"

From `'PTSD Nation - The New 'ism for a New Generation'` (pp. 35-36) by Jerry Barnes, Ph.D., Ed.D., former M.D.

"And now, Good Reader, you ask another $50,000 question. Why are these guys (and girls- remember G.I. Jane too folks) so sensitive?

Because they are pissed! Angry, most professionals call it. But the vets would agree more with my verbiage.

Those of us in the mental health business know that anger is most often rooted in fear.

So what is it they fear you ask (your points are adding up player)? There are no bombs here and no one is shooting at them now, hopefully, and in most cases.

More than anything, what they fear is loss of control. Remember, while they were in the hell of war, they were also in the highly controlled environment of the U.S. military machine, which is more controlled than our prison systems or any dictatorship or other form of government on earth. 'This is not a democracy' is one of the favorite mantras screamed repeatedly by those in charge.

A prison system mentality quickly develops among the troops, and for the lower ranking soldiers, Stockholm syndrome soon follows. This is the "ism" (God I love that label) where hostages express empathy toward their captors. And you see Good Reader, during a soldier's deployment their chain of command and the almighty Department of Defense *are* their captors.

Every need the soldier has is dependent upon the actions of their superiors (captors); food, clothing and shelter- a shoulder to cry on, the ability to make sure things are going well back home.

Well, Good Reader, among our military ranks there are many captors who do not notice that Stockholm syndrome has developed among some of their troops and the importance and delicacy with which this situation must be handled. Throw a couple of men or women of rank in the picture whose power has gone to their head (aforementioned prison mentality, also known as toxic leadership) and you have a mix for disaster.

Many soldiers have come back from the fronts in the Middle East and reported terrible treatment from their leadership. Not physical per say, though many were physically abused, but mental and emotional.

Soldiers have been going without being allowed to eat, and some have been going without pay. That's right, Good Reader, we have boys and girls over there fighting for free. Or at least 'on loan' for now as our government will eventual pay them, generally before a formal complaint goes too high up the chain.

Of course, they may end up being killed fist.

They are going without the 'reasonable' ability to stay in touch with family back home. Sure, this isn't a luxury typically enjoyed in the history of war, but with modern technology that even a near ninety year old coot such as myself can and does use, and now that the wars, especially the one in Iraq, have become occupations, there should be ample time to stay in touch with folks back home, and most of the troops do.

And so, the anger we see from our vets after coming home is most often rooted in the fear of losing control, or being controlled by others again; reliving the hell. And it pisses them off!

So, next time you are working at the factory or in the shop or down at the convenient store and you tell a coworker who happens to be a vet to grab a broom and start sweeping, you might want to say 'please.'

7

*Meeting between Jennifer Hutton (L.C.S.W.) and Corey Prine- December 6, 2009

"You look like crap, Corey," Jennifer said, leading Corey from the waiting area to her office.

"Thanks," he said. His voice was hoarse, and his eyes were red, as if he hadn't slept, or as if he'd done so in a drunken stupor. He hadn't shaved in at least a week.

"No, seriously," she said, closing the door to her office, motioning him to sit. "What's going on? You weren't too happy when you left her last time. What's happened in the past month?" She walked behind her desk and sat down.

"It's been a rough couple of weeks," he said, rubbing his tired, burning eyes.

"What's gone on in the past couple of weeks?"

"Well, a couple things really. Mail. It's all come in the mail. Same day."

Oh shit Jen, he's been denied.

"What's come in the mail, Corey?"

"Well, first I got a letter from the VA claims office."

"And?" she said, holding her breath.

"And I got denied."

"On what?"

"On everything."

"No way," she said, leaning forward, eyes wide. "No way! If you don't have PTSD no one does! And your hearing. The tinnitus. And your back. How could…"

"Exactly," he said. "But it gets better."

"How so?"

"I also got a letter from the great state of California, that same day, telling me I'm behind on child support. Six months behind at $700 a month!"

"What?"

"There was a number, so I called it. Basically, some woman on the other end tells me that she cannot tell me anything about the whereabouts of my son and ex wife and that my support amount is based on my income while I was deployed, my last job."

"But you aren't working now," Jennifer said. "And you don't even know where your son is."

"She said none of that mattered, and that if I didn't get caught up on support a warrant would be issued for my arrest. I'd get picked up in West Virginia and prosecuted under California law."

"Oh my God," Jennifer said, leaning back in her chair. "Please tell me you didn't do anything stupid that day."

"Depends on what you call stupid," he said.

"Come on Corey. Tell me what you did."

"I went out and got blind fuckin' drunk!"

"Corey!" she shouted, sitting forward again. "You know that is only going to make things worse!"

"Some ways yes. Some ways no," he said.

"In what way could drinking help anything? We've talked about this. You are going to give yourself more problems. You told me once before that you felt you had an addictive personality. Do you want another monkey on your back?"

"My back, Jennifer. That is exactly how it helps. My back!"

"What?"

"I went out and started chugging some beers and bam! Three beers into a binge, and my back didn't hurt anymore. I've slept a lot better ever since too."

"Are you drinking every night?"

"Yes," he said. "And though the hangovers suck, the sleep is wonderful. Finally, I can sleep."

"Oh shit," she said, leaning back. She rubbed her own eyes now, collecting her thoughts. "Corey, if I can get you something for your back, will you stop drinking? This is going nowhere but bad."

"More meds," he said, sarcastically.

"Obviously you need something."

"But won't I get hooked on that shit?"

Poor Richards, he thought, an image of Richard's smiling, pre-drug addicted face in his head.

"No," she said. "I mean sure, everyone knows there's tens of thousands of vets out there hooked on Vicodin and Percocet. But lately we've been giving out Tramadol. It's non-narcotic. Habit forming yes, but addictive, no."

"So you have the guy down the hall give it to me? Like the Citalopram?"

"No," she said. "Who is your PA?"

"Janet somebody."

"Jan Scholls?"

"Yeah, that's her."

"Sit tight," Jennifer said, reaching for her phone. She made a call and ten minutes later Corey's P.A. was sitting in the office with them.

"So, what's going on with you, kid?" she asked. Janet, or Jan as everyone at the VA called her, was in her late fifties, though you'd never know by looking at her. She was an avid distance runner and had the energy of a young child. It wasn't uncommon for her to be accused of being her thirty year old daughter's sister. She'd been with the VA for a quarter of a century, and like Jennifer, Corey liked her and trusted her.

"I've been boozin' it up," he said. "'Cause my back hurts and it seems to be the only way I can get to sleep."

"Ah," Jan said. "Self medicating."

"If that's what you call it."

"That's what we call it kiddo."

Jennifer spoke next. "I've told Corey that Tramadol might be appropriate. We want to stay away from narcotics because he's admitted to having an addictive personality."

"Here's the deal," Jan said, looking Corey in the eyes sternly. "I'll write the script, but you must stop drinking. And no other drug use. We'll treat you the right way."

"With U.S. Government engineered pharmaceuticals?" he asked.

"With U.S. Government backed pharmaceuticals," Jan said. "They didn't make them. They just use them. Agreed?"

"Sure," Corey said. He didn't sound committed.

"I mean it, kiddo. You keep drinking or start smoking pot and you're coming off these things."

"Ok," he said, serious now.

"Don't worry," Jan said. "They're free, like everything else here."

"Not exactly," Jennifer said, looking over at Jan. "He's been denied on his claim."

"My God," Jan said, throwing her head back and rolling her eyes. "Look kid. Most vets are at first. You have to appeal. They'll give you something on the appeal. Especially when they see you are on Tramadol."

"How do I appeal?" Corey asked. "How long does that take?"

"Here," Jennifer said, pulling a business card out of her desk drawer and handing it across the desk to Corey. "Here's the number of the lawyer (fucking lawyers, the voice of Dr. Barnes' whispered in her mind) who handles most of my vet's cases. She's good. She'll get you at least fifty percent, but that will take up to a year. She'll appeal that decision also, and within two to five years she'll get you what you rightly deserve."

"You have got to be fuckin' kidding me!" Corey said. "They didn't give me two to five years to get my ass over to Iraq! They gave me ninety fuckin' days."

"Look Corey," Jennifer said, now handing him a form she'd printed while he was comparing the time frames in which the government acts on behalf of its people, and the time frame in which the people are expected to act on behalf of their government. "This is a 'financial hardship' form. I'll help you fill it out and I'll hand deliver it to finance. You aren't working so they won't charge you for the Tramadol. And without this hardship request form they'll want to come back and charge you for the Citalopram you've gotten already since your claim has been denied."

"Fuckin' commies!" he said.

"Welcome back to the U.S. of A., kiddo," Jan said, rising to her feet. "I'll shoot your script over to the pharmacy. I've got an appointment, gotta go!"

And with that she was gone, as if someone had fired a starter's pistol at the beginning of one of the many 10k road races she ran almost every weekend.

Corey leaned back in his chair as the door closed. He felt as if he'd gotten another letter with bad news.

"Let's talk, Corey."

"About what?" he said, looking up as Jennifer spoke.

"About how I'm feeling like you're a time bomb waiting to go off."

She sat back in her chair, waiting for him to open up, but he didn't. He retreated somewhere inside of himself, his eyes took on that same crazed look as before that had always made her skin crawl.

Fuck a penny. I'd give the U.S. mint for his thoughts. This is not good, Jen. Not good at all.

*

*From the personal diary of Jennifer Hutton- December 9, 2009

Poor Corey Prine. He's all I could think about at the gym, the fastest hour on the lifecycle I've ever spent.

This guy keeps getting screwed by everyone. The Army, his ex-wife, the state of California demanding support for a kid he hasn't seen since he was three months old.

And now the VA.

I'm afraid that at some point, someone else is going to be sorry for all of this. I'm just not sure who, or when.

I've scheduled him to come back in the middle of the month. The holidays are coming up and that is always a tough time for vets. Hell, for everyone. And it is a tough time for me.

God I miss my daddy.

I am such a mess. I really need to go see Dr. Barnes again. But I really don't know if it is for help with Corey or for me.

Good night, Dearest Diary.

*

From 'PTSD Nation – The New 'ism for a New Generation' (pp. 42-45) by Jerry Barnes, Ph.D., Ed.D., former M.D.

"Delay, deny and hope that I die!" This, Good Reader, has become a common phrase believed to be truth among too many of our veterans who have filed claims for disabilities with the VA.

And what is behind the origination of this morbid statement? Time, Good Reader. Time.

The phrase is pretty self explanatory, but to make it clearer for you, it means this; from the time a vet files his or her original claim with the VA, it takes one year on average to get a response. If the vet disagrees with the response and files an appeal, the average length of time in which their dispute will be concluded is four years. Hence the now too common expression stated above. "Delay, deny and hope that I die!"

Many veterans, even those suffering from physical injury, and who bear visible scars from I.E.D. explosions, small arms fire, or non-combat related injuries are being denied by the hundreds of thousands because they cannot "prove" when, where, why, and how the incident took place.

Story after story tells of vets who are already receiving small percentages of disability for, say, an injury caused by an I.E.D., but when they apply for compensation based on PTSD, the VA, who, again, is already paying them for a physical injury due to the injurious event, rejects the claim for PTSD because of the vets inability to prove the event took place.

Confusing? You betcha!

Now remember, Good Reader, shortly into their year in hell (deployment it's called), the days and nights quickly run together and become the same for these men and women in our armed services. Even in what little down time they have, most would be hard pressed to tell you what day of the week it is.

And, perhaps the 'witnesses' the VA so heavily seeks (they are not calling the vet a liar per-say, only insinuating that the vet is lying) cannot be found because they did not survive the event. Perhaps they have been one of the thousands upon thousands who have committed suicide (delay, deny and hope that I die) since returning from war. And to go back even further, to veterans who are still fighting claims from Vietnam, Korea and WWII, YES EVEN- WWII, chances are, any witnesses that made it through the war and suicidal tendencies they may have had following the war, have died of old age.

This obviously makes our vets feel more alienated. But don't take it personal G.I. Joe and G.I. Jane, because it isn't personal. It's merely a numbers game, not a people game.

Currently, the VA has nearly one million disability claims on backlog. Though they've done well in recent years to hire more people and throw more money at the problem, this backlog has only gotten bigger.

So, in their 'infinite wisdom' the leaders at the VA in charge of claims have set up a points system. The more claims you clear from the backlog, the more points you as a VA employee earn toward bonuses and promotions.

As you might imagine, the focus then becomes, under such a points system, not the veteran, but the clearing of claims. And the mountain of claims in front of you can be cleared more quickly by pulling out your big rubber "denied" stamp, pounding it down with fresh ink on page one of the claim in front of you, and then moving on to do the same with the next claim, rather than by being thorough and making sure that the few who have done so much to protect so many are treated squarely.

'Welcome home soldier!'

For so many who have deposited so much into their Nation's bank account, not through funds but through blood, sweat and tears; through the loss of relationships, the loss of physical and mental health, it seems as if it is so hard, if not next to impossible, to make a withdrawal.

8

*Meeting between Jennifer Hutton (L.C.S.W.) and Corey Prine- December 15, 2009

"How have you been over the last two weeks, Corey?" Jennifer asked.

Corey thought Jennifer seemed apprehensive, but he wasn't sure, because he was stoned out of his mind.

"Okay," he said.

"Have you been taking your Tramadol?"

Boy, have I, he thought.

"Yes," he said.

"And have you been staying off the booze?" she asked.

"Yes," he said, and it wasn't a lie. He hadn't drunk in more than twenty four hours. But before that, he was drinking like a fish. Enough to float the navy of a third world nation.

He'd discovered quickly that Tramadol and alcohol was a great mix. The Tramadol was free due to his hardship claim filed with the VA, and it greatly lowered his alcohol expenses.

He'd been quite the chemist over the past couple of weeks, working on the perfect mix. The ideal combination seemed to be one Tramadol for every two beers. It doubled the effects of the booze, allowing him to get the desired buzz for only half the price.

With no VA disability money coming in and no job, he had to save money on his drink. His cousin had already quit at the pallet mill; too much work for his fat ass, Corey thought, but *again,* Mr. Lupshin had *not* kept him in mind and had not called him.

So the day before the current session, Corey's goal had been to avoid alcohol so that Jennifer wouldn't smell anything on his breath.

And take away his Tramadol.

They cannot stop prescribing me this stuff, he thought, remembering Jan's threat. *It is manna from heaven!*

So around noon he'd doubled up on his pills. *Can't smell these*, he thought as he'd popped them. *And to hell with lunch anyway,* he'd also thought. *Food kills your buzz.*

Then, just before dinner, he'd tripled up on the pills
(more exponentially so, if you counted the fact that he was
supposed to have waited a couple more hours before taking more).

But dinner had killed his buzz (*told you so*), so shortly
after that he quadrupled his intake. He threw in a couple
Citalopram on top of it all around ten p.m. and slept like a
baby.

And then, of course, he had loaded up before his
appointment today. He wanted to be calm; give the impression
that it was *all good*.

"Good," she said, relieved. "Have you calmed down about the
whole claim denial thing some?"

"Oh yea," he said. "Water under the bridge."

With enough Tramadol and booze, he thought, *it's all water
under the bridge.*

"What are your plans for the holidays?"

Tramadol and alcohol, he thought.

"I don't have any really," he said.

"You won't be alone will you?" she asked

God, *I don't want to be alone again,* Jennifer thought.

"I mean, you'll at least be with your parents, right?"

"Oh yea," he said.

If I come down, he thought. *Pun intended.*

"You're not going to be alone are you, Jennifer?" he asked.

Is he reading my mind again?

"Nothing personal, Corey, but I really go out of my way to
avoid discussing my personal life with my vets. Not a good idea,
ya know."

"Sorry," he said. "Just, no ring on your finger. No
pictures of kids or some dude here in your office."

"You are very observant," she said.

Even through the haze, he thought. *Oh, this wonderful, wonderful haze!*

"Had to be to stay alive over there," he said.

"Christmas is tough for me, Corey."

Why did I tell him that?

"And why is that, Jennifer?" he asked.

"I lost my father when I was young. I was only four."

And why in the hell did I tell him that?

"That's terrible," he said. Becoming privy to this aspect of Jennifer's life drew him out of the haze a little, almost as if he'd eaten food. "I'm sorry to hear that."

"Car crash," she said. "Well, tractor trailer crash."

Stop now Jen! Stop now! her mind was screaming.

"He got hit by a tractor trailer?" Corey asked, his buzz almost gone now, diminishing more with each new piece of the story.

"No," she said. "He drove tractor trailer on the west coast. It was winter time, not long after Christmas. He went off the road and over a cliff on the pass through the Cascades above Seattle."

"Wow," he said. "I really *am* sorry to hear that." And he was, and his buzz was now completely gone.

"Yeah," she said, shrugging and looking away, her guard completely down.

Why not let it all out? she thought.

"It's always hardest around Christmas, ya know. One of the few memories I even have of him is of that last Christmas together. There are more, but that one seems to stick out the most.

"I just remember dancing and dancing with Christmas music playing. He'd swing me around and we'd both laugh until we cried. I still have lots of pictures."

There was a long silence in the room. Jennifer was lost in time, her eyes turned down toward her desk, but she wasn't seeing it.

Corey had turned his head while listening and begun watching the snow come down outside the window. He had missed home all the years he had lived in Virginia, and he had especially missed it the year he was in Iraq, but he had never missed the snow.

"I'm sorry, Corey," Jennifer finally said. "This isn't about me. This is about you."

"It's ok, Jennifer."

But fuck! You killed my buzz!

"He was in Vietnam," she said, barely audible.

"What?" Corey said, turning to face her.

"My dad. He was in Vietnam. He had been in the Army before I was born. He was a combat veteran."

"Oh," Corey said, making the connection. "Is that why you do what you do?"

"Kinda," she said. "Not entirely. But I do think it is why I prefer to work with vets. It reminds me of the dad I never really knew. Makes me feel like I'm helping him in spirit by helping others like him."

"Oh," he said

"But back to you," she said.

My God I can't believe I just told him all that stuff, she thought.

"I'll be fine, Jennifer," he said, waving his hand. "I've decided to give myself a Christmas gift that'll be handy after the New Year."

"What's that?"

"A driver's license. I'm going to go to the DMV and do whatever I have to do to renew it."

"That's great, Corey!" she said, and her face lit up, the look of borderline depression disappearing. "I'm so proud of you! It shows that you are coping better. Dealing with your responsibilities."

"Got to some time," he said.

God I want a pill. Or a drink. Or both! he thought.

"You know, getting you in here today I think helped me more than it helped you," she said.

"Glad to help," he said.

God, has it been an hour yet, he thought.

"So, back to your claim," she said. "Have you contacted the lawyer yet to file an appeal?"

"Not yet," he said.

Just tell her anything and get the hell out of here goddamn it!

"I plan to after the New Year. I know I'm due *something* from the VA. It isn't some false pride issue I'm struggling with about getting the money. I mean, I'll take all I can get (*especially more Tramadol if you would, please*) but for now I think I'll stay more motivated to renew my license if I'm not sitting around waiting on the money to come in."

"Look at you," she said, all smiles. "You've gotten such a positive attitude. Isn't it amazing what several good nights of sleep strung together can do? And staying sober?"

"Yes," he said. But he knew that the reason he was sleeping so well as of late was because he *wasn't* staying sober.

"And now, what about those thoughts?" she asked. "You know I have to ask, Corey. I haven't looked at your intake form today, so level with me. Are you feeling suicidal or homicidal?"

"Not at all," he said, but he was thinking that he was going to kill somebody if he didn't eat some more Tramadol soon.

"Great! If you keep this up, Corey, I think we'll make you the poster child of the VA."

"Great," he said, shifting uncomfortably in his chair. "Hey, why don't you say we knock off a bit early today? Looks like its piling up out there." He nodded toward the window. Her eyes followed. "I'm the only one the VA van brought today, so we can leave when I'm done. You know, they have all those old guys driving those things. I don't trust 'em so much on the back roads when the snow's on."

"Yeah, you're right. I think you get a star beside your name today. I'll be seeing you again after the holidays, I guess."

"Can't wait," he said, but what he really couldn't wait to do was get his hands on the pills in his pants pocket.

After printing off and handing him his next appointment slip, Jennifer walked him to the door that separated the counselor's offices from the lobby. She told him to have a great Christmas and New Year, and then she turned and went back into the hall, pulling the door closed behind her.

He went directly to the water fountain outside of the restrooms. No one was around so he didn't even try to conceal the act of pulling six Tramadol pills out of his pants pocket and then popping them in his mouth and chasing them down with water.

And then he went out into the snow.

* VA computer system notes of Jennifer Hutton

December 15, 2009

Met with C. Prine today. Doing great! Recently began taking Tramadol and reports sleeping better due to lack of back pain. Still taking Citalopram. Reports that he is not drinking and that he plans to spend the holidays with his parents. Seems to be making great progress overall.

*

*Personal diary entry of Jennifer Hutton, December 15, 2009

Dearest Diary,

I am such a mess. God did I screw up today. I bled my heart out to Corey. I don't know why. Yes, it made me feel better, but it was so unprofessional of me. I have *never* done anything like that with *any* of my vets before.

But God, I just feel like I had to talk to somebody. That's the hardest part about what I do, always hearing about everyone else's issues and never venting my own.

Oh, I know I could. They have help for us at the VA. But anything we tell those bitches gets spread all over the break room so I just keep it all in.

And then I get diarrhea of the mouth with a patient today.

Rob's been calling. I haven't seen him since last week. The man can make me feel so good physically, but then ruin it all as soon as he opens his mouth afterward. What a prick!

Pardon the wet spots on your pages, Dearest Diary. I can't help crying. I was worried about Corey and my other vets. How they'd spend their holidays. But all I keep thinking about now is me and my miserable, single existence.

And my daddy.

I haven't even been able to bring myself to pull out the albums and look at the pictures in a couple of years. I feel them calling to me but I just can't go to them.

I'm calling Dr. Barnes tomorrow. He can help.

Good night, Dearest Diary.

9

Meeting between Jennifer Hutton (L.C.S.W.) and Jerry Barnes, Ph.D., Ed.d., former M.D. December 18, 2009

"So, have you come seeking advice for a patient or for a personal session, dear?" Dr. Barnes asked Jennifer as she sat in the overstuffed chair in his den. She paid little attention to the elves hats his hired assistants were wearing, no doubt part of the required, perverted uniform for the season.

"What do you mean?" she asked, knowing she couldn't bullshit this old bullshitter.

"Your eyes are so red and puffy," he said, taking a *not* so innocent glance at his lovely assistant's back side as she left the room and shut the door behind her. "It looks like you've been crying for days."

"I have been," she said, taking in a deep breath, followed by a long, resigning exhale. "I've been upset for days. It's the season. Christmas is always hard."

"So what's happened, dear?" he said, and then he nestled the thin air line coming out of his nose into the most comfortable spot he could, and in which he hoped it would stay. He placed his hands under the afghan on his lap and said, "Let's dance."

"I saw Corey Prine again a few days ago," she said, pulling a fresh Kleenex out of her purse in anticipation of the tears she could feel coming. "And I got diarrhea of the mouth about my own problems. And I've never done anything like that with a patient before, so I know something is going on with me, and I need to get help or I'm no good to anyone."

And then she let the tears flow.

"So what is *really* bothering you, dear?" he asked, taking his hands out from under the afghan and then rolling toward her. He took one of her hands in both of his once he got there.

She looked up, eyes like a puppy.

"I miss my daddy," she said, and a fresh onset of tears came forth.

"Do you miss your father Jen, or do you miss the idea of a father?"

"What?" she said, confusion in her voice.

"We've talked about this before. Just never in detail because you've always chosen to skirt around the issue."

He released her hand and wheeled himself back a few feet.

"Every therapist has a reason they enter this business, Jennifer, an Achilles heel so to say, and yours is your father. But what confuses me, is whether or not it is actually your father, the man, or your father, the idea."

Jennifer wiped snot from under her nose. She'd stopped crying now, her feelings sobered by the line of questioning.

"How old were you when your father died?"

"I was only four," she said, repositioning in her chair.

"How many memories could you have of the man?" Dr. Barnes asked. "And how close to reality could they be? A blurb here, a blurb there. And perhaps no way to put any of the blurbs into the context of any real situation that may have occurred at the time. Simply the memories of a little girl, snap shots in a photo album. Nothing more."

"I guess you're right," she said, looking down at her hands. She watched the ends of her fingers anxiously kneed the half used tissue she held, as if each finger had a mind of its own.

"Then perhaps it's the issue of never knowing what it was like to have a father that bothers you. Your mother never remarried, isn't that correct?"

"Yes. That's right."

"How much have you talked to your mother about your father?"

"In recent years?" she asked.

"Ever."

"Not much at all."

"And why is that, Jennifer?" He turned his head and glanced out the steamed window. It wasn't snowing now, but there was a good ten inches accumulated on the ground. There would be much more to come over the next two months, and the older he got the harder it was for him to tolerate the winters in West Virginia. *Should've started going south like everyone else, twenty years ago,* he thought.

"She never wanted to talk about him," she said, looking down, recalling memories. "Anytime I would say anything about him, she would ignore me. If I pressed the issue, she'd get upset."

"Why do you think she acted this way, Jennifer?"

"I always assumed that it hurt her just as much to be without him as it did me. More so, I came to realize as I got older. She had actually known him. She'd had a relationship with him that she could remember." She paused and looked out the same window he was and into the snow. "She had actually known him," she said, almost inaudibly.

"You've told me that he was a Vietnam veteran," he said.

"That's right," she said.

"And that he died in a tractor trailer accident."

"Yes."

"Do you believe this dear, that it really was an accident, with all of the things you know about vets after having worked with them for so long?"

She glanced down at her hands again, saying nothing. She'd asked herself this question in the past, but she'd always dismissed it as quickly as her mother had always dismissed the issue of her father.

"What are your plans for Christmas, dear?" Dr. Barnes said.

"I have none, really," she said, looking up and meeting his eyes. "Are you looking for some company?"

"Oh no," he said, chuckling. "The girls are dressing up like little elves and entertaining me all day." He grinned in anticipation. "I was simply going to suggest that you spend some time with your mother."

"In Washington?" she said, surprised.

"Has she relocated?"

"No, but…"

"I think it's time you put a brace on that Achilles heel of yours, young lady."

"So you are suggesting I fly to Washington and bring up the ghosts of Christmas past with my mother? Now that I'm almost forty?"

"Yes. But not now that you are almost forty. It should have been done years ago. But rather, now, while your mother is still among the living and the opportunity is here to be had."

Jennifer sat in silence, staring back down at her hands. It was now as if her fingers had their own ears and had heard this suggestion and stopped kneading the Kleenex.

"It's the only way you will ever be free, Jennifer. And like you said yourself, while you're a mess, you are no good to anyone, especially any of your patients who need you. You need to deal with their 'isms and you cannot do that objectively if you haven't dealt with your own."

"You're right," she said, looking up to meet his eyes again. "And this is something I've known I've needed to do for a long time. I've just lied to myself and put it off."

"Those of us in the business are the best at doing just that, dear. We have so many big textbook terms that we can give as our justifications for doing so. Like the word 'justification' itself. But the only way to heal is by walking through the fire."

"Thank you, Dr. Barnes," she said, rising. "I'm going home to get online. I'm going to book the first flight to Sea-Tac on the twenty first. I'm not wasting any more time." She began walking toward the door.

"Jen," he said, pulling up behind her in his wheelchair. She turned, realizing she'd not bid him a proper farewell.

"Sorry," she said, reaching down and taking both of his outstretched hands in her own. "Thank you so much and have a wonderful Christmas."

"How is that patient of yours?" he asked, ignoring her pleasantries. "The one you came to see me about before, Mr. Prine?"

"Oh, he's fine," she said. "He's still on Citalopram, and we've got him on Tramadol for his back pain now. So he seems to be stabilizing."

"More meds."

"Yes," she said, averting his eyes. She felt as if *he* felt she had taken a short cut.

"Anything else about this guy that makes you uneasy? Anything that makes you feel like he could climb a tower and start shooting at the people passing by below?"

She hesitated for a long time before saying no. But Dr. Barnes, the bullshitter not to be bullshitted, knew exactly what the pause had meant.

It meant that Jennifer Hutton had no clue what Corey Prine was capable of doing and what he just might do.

"Have a safe flight and a good trip, dear," he said, giving both of her hands a gingerly squeeze before letting them go. "Let me know when you get back. Perhaps then we'll finish the dance."

"I can't wait," she said, smiling, and then she turned and left.

Dr. Barnes rolled himself to the large bay window and stared out into the snow. The sun was beginning to set behind a curtain of clouds, giving the gray and white outside an eerie glow.

He rolled back over to his desk and took a key out of the thin center drawer. With it, he opened the large drawer on the bottom right of the desk and took out an old photo album.

He opened the album to the first page, a news article announcing the suicidal death of Vietnam veteran Reginald "Reggie" Jones, found dead in his home after eating a piece of lead from the business end of a .38.

Reggie had been one of Dr. Barnes' patients. *He* had actually been the first patient Dr. Barnes had ever treated who had committed suicide, back in 1968. The first had *not* been the vet who had gone bungee jumping without a chord from the New River Gorge back in the late 1990's.

And Reggie had only been the first of many.

He began flipping through the news articles and pictures in the album. So many faces, so many memories rushing through his mind.

He dropped the book to the floor, grabbing at the sharp piercing pain in his chest with a clenching left hand. He felt for the air tube in his nose with his right hand. It hadn't fallen out, it was still there, yet the pain in his chest was there too, and he was finding it hard to breathe.

He began to panic, rolling slowly toward the door. Reaching it, he grabbed the knob and twisted it, opening the door to scream for help. But as the door opened the pain receded, and then it was gone.

Had it ever really been there at all?

#

After arriving home, Jennifer had gotten online to book her flight to the west coast before even taking the time to breathe and convince herself that it might be best to call her mother first and make her aware of her plan to visit.

Calm down, Jen. The old girl isn't going anywhere. She never goes anywhere.

She made herself a cup of chamomile tea and sat on the couch, letting the laptop fall asleep on the coffee table. Half way through the mug of hot comfort, she pulled out an old photo album sitting on the bottom shelf of the bookcase beside the couch, an album she hadn't touched in three years.

The first picture she noticed was the one she had always stared at while always drinking too much wine or beer on too many Christmas Eves. The one of her, at four years old, sitting on her father's lap back in Washington. He was wearing a Santa hat and holding her with both arms wrapped tightly around her. They were both smiling with tears in their eyes.

We danced and laughed until we cried, she thought.

And then she saw something she'd seen hundreds of times in the past, but seemed to be noticing for the first time only now.

His eyes.

Oh my God! Those eyes!

She dropped her mug, and it fell over on the floor, spilling the rest of its contents onto the carpet.

Those are Corey's eyes!

9

*From the Personal Diary of Jennifer Hutton- December 21, 2009

Dearest Diary,

Here I am, leaving on a jet plane. But I *do* know when I'll be back again. New Year's day.

The flight's been fine so far. I'm fortunate to be seated between what appears to be two businessmen who are content to look at spread sheets and charts on their laptops and leave me alone.

And they are both thin.

I tried reading the new Ron Adam's novel, "Lake Effect," and though it's quick paced and mind bending like his other novels, it just couldn't hold my attention. But only because my mind is in so many different places right now. Oh, where to start?

I'll start with mom, the reason for the trip. Well, really dad is the reason for the trip, but you know what I mean.

I really do love my mother, and I am excited to see her. God, it's been four years. And I have so much respect for her. She never remarried after my father died and to be honest, I'm not even sure if she ever even dated.

Two memories about my mother stand out most. She was always working, and she never wanted to talk about my father.

She put in so many hours as a custodian at U.W., all those overtime hours on the weekends working the stadiums after football games or in the arena after basketball games.

But other than being gone at work a lot she was always there for me in every other way. All my needs were met. There was never a time when I was hungry and couldn't eat.

We kept a clean, orderly little house in Belmont. And our cars (we only had two during my years growing up) were always clean and tidy and kept up. Mom never made much money and she knew it was cheaper to keep the oil changed and the bolts and nuts lubed than it was to replace a car, so she did.

But we never really bonded. It was more like we were roommates, not mother and daughter.

And I guess she got lucky with me as her daughter, because I was never wild. I was never one to run around with boys, fogging up the windows in parked cars on the weekends. But boy did I make up for that when I got to college. All those notes are safely tucked away in the reams of some of your predecessors, Dearest Diary.

It never really bothered me at the time that we didn't bond like in all those movies on the Hallmark Channel. What a bunch of fake ass crap that stuff is anyway. But, when nothing else is on…

But it *always* bothered me when I asked about my father and she took the attitude that the man had never existed.

Knowing what I know now, as a big girl nearing forty whose spent fifteen years in the mental health industry ('business' as Dr. Barnes would call it), I can see that she was simply repressing her own memories and feelings. It was the hardest thing she had ever gone through also, and she didn't like to dig up the demons so to say.

So maybe this trip will be as healing for her as it will be for me. Maybe there is a God, and he (or she or it) has a plan, and this has all been part of that plan; my chosen field, time away from my mother to put it all in perspective, dealing with veterans so I can relate to living with them as a family member. It seems clearer to me now than it ever has.

And that's another story; veterans. Particularly one named Corey Prine.

I felt like I had really gotten in tune with him, like I was sitting in his head and could really see what was going on with him. And then I had my little meltdown, right in front of him, completely ignoring what was going on with him and at such a vulnerable time for him.

He'd just been turned down on his VA claim, he's been struggling with alcohol, and we've just put him on a regimen of meds. God, do I feel like I took a major short cut with that. And not to mention, it's Christmas. Suicide and homicide rates jump through the roof this time of year, especially among vets.

But I can understand the Tramadol. I mean, these guys are coming back from over there with their backs totally destroyed from that body armor they have to wear. And its common sense, even if you aren't in the mental healthcare field, that if you can't get a good night's sleep, you're going to be a mess. Add to that all the other things these guys have been through and it is a recipe for disaster.

And on a side note, it pisses me off that they could be protected with armor that weighs half as much as what they have to wear now. The problem is that it costs twice as much and big government isn't going to spend that much money on enlisted men. Better to give it to those contractors to divvy up among themselves.

God, Dearest Diary, I am thankful to have you as an outlet. The things I tell you that I can't tell any others. If I put this stuff in my notes at work I'd be blackballed for sure.

And God knows Rob would never listen. He'd call me a whiner or a cry baby like he does my vets.

So that brings up, lastly, and a distant lastly, Rob. Not much news there, and I feel there will be less going forward. In spite of having so much on my mind, I have been tossing around some preliminary ideas for a New Year's resolution list. And one of the habits I think I want to break is Mr. Robbo.

Anyway, I've been informed by the guy in the sky (the pilot, not the God that may or may not be) that we are ready to descend into Seattle. So for now, I wish you goodbye and a very Merry Christmas.

Wish me luck, Dearest Diary.

From 'PTSD Nation – The New 'ism for a New Generation' (pp. 63-64) by Jerry Barnes, Ph.D., Ed.D., former M.D.

We all know that the holidays bring not only cheer and merriment, or at least they are supposed to, but also for many people, depression, anger and deep feelings of guilt and loss.

As stated before, the biggest, most identifiable traits of Post Traumatic Stress Disorder are one's inability to cope and depression. Now, add to this condition the holidays; a time of year in which the rates of suicide and domestic violence among the civilian population sky rockets due to unwanted memories and undesirable current circumstances and then consider our vets.

And keep an eye on them.

If they seem as if they are going to hurt themselves there is a good chance that they probably are, so you should call for help.

And if they seem as if they are dead set on hurting someone else?

Get the hell out of their way!

11

The first three days that passed between Jennifer and her mother, Helen, did so as if the hours were being shared between two acquaintances that had reunited after a long parting, not mother and daughter.

"I like what you've done with the house," was the type of commonly courteous comments Jennifer made to her mother.

"I like how you are keeping your hair these days," was a similarly simple, commonly courteous type of remark from her mother.

Translated, three days passed that were filled with empty words in which nothing of any substance was said.

Until Christmas Eve.

"That was a great dinner," Jennifer said and then lifted her glass of warm spiced wine to her lips. The dismal conversation had moved from the small dining room table that took up half of the small kitchen to the equally small living room.

"So why are you really here?" Helen asked, ending the empty nuances. Jennifer nearly choked on her hot tottie, shocked by both her mother's frankness, surely encouraged by the wine, and a flashback of her last conversation with Dr. Barnes at the same time.

"It's Christmas," she said, hoping that her mother hadn't noticed her brief loss of composure. "It's been years since we've seen each other."

"You're right," her mother said. "It *has* been years. Four years." She poured more wine, now quickly cooling to room temperature into her glass and then sat the bottle back on the coffee table between them. "Why now?"

Jennifer sat in silence, unable to meet her mother's eyes.

"It's your father, isn't it?"

Jennifer looked up.

"I'm not upset," her mother said, smiling. "Promise, I'm not. You're almost forty. I'm surprised it's taken you this long to come around, and I'll tell you anything you want to know."

Jennifer took another sip of her wine before speaking, buying time and building courage. When she did speak, she said, "So why so willing now, mom? You never seemed interested in talking about him in the past. You always changed the subject."

"You were too young to hear the truth when you were a kid," Helen said, putting her glass on the table and then crossing her hands across her lap. "And you let it go once you were in college, but I knew the time would come when you'd come back to the questions. And it's only fair to you that I answer them. And that I answer them honestly.

"But I guess part of me secretly hoped you'd never ask," she said, almost whispering, and then she picked up her glass and swallowed the rest of her wine in one gulp. "But you *had* to go into counseling," she said, waving her hand beside her head, as if swatting away a mosquito that wasn't there. "And then there *had* to be another Vietnam, and you *had* to start working with the psychos coming back from this one."

"Mother," Jennifer said, jutting forward in her seat.

"It's true," her mother said. Her voice was calm in spite of Jennifer's reaction. "It's not their fault. Nobody's blaming them, it's just true.

"But anyway, do you want to know the truth about your hero? Your father? Or do you want to wait another forty years? But I probably won't be here to give it to you then if you do."

Jennifer leaned back into the couch and breathed deeply, allowing her heart rate to slow. She said nothing, because she knew not what to say.

"Fire away," her mother said.

"The accident," Jennifer said, finally. "Was it really an accident?"

"No," Helen said with no hesitation, her face as straight as an arrow.

"You have no doubt?"

"None whatsoever and I never did."

Jennifer was speechless in light of the non-sugar coated truth.

"Your father killed himself, Jennifer."

"But… but…" Jennifer stammered, looking at the empty space between her outstretched hands as if there was something there to see.

"Because he didn't want to spend his life in prison for killing someone else," her mother said, answering the 'why' that Jennifer hadn't been able to ask.

"But I don't get it," Jennifer said. "Who would he have killed? Why?"

"You already know the answers, Jennifer. You've been working with guys just like your dad for years. Don't be so naive to think that he was any different than the rest of these pissed off psychos that are nothing more than burdens on the state and time bombs waiting to go off."

"Mother!" She sat forward in her seat again. "How can you say that?"

"Listen. I don't know why you came here, if it wasn't for the truth. Now can you handle it? Here," she said, taking the bottle of wine from the coffee table and handing it to Jennifer. "Maybe you need more of this."

"Yeah," Jennifer said, taking the bottle and then pouring herself a fresh glass of wine. "And maybe you don't." She raised her glass as if making a toast and then chugged its entire contents. Afterward, she poured another glass and did the same.

Several minutes of silence passed in which Jennifer let what her mother had told her and the alcohol content of the wine sink in before speaking again.

"Where there signs of any of this?" Jennifer asked, her voice letting her mother know that her initial shock was gone and that, yes, she was now ready for the truth.

"Signs?" Helen said and then threw her head back with near maniacal laughter. "He was facing ten years in prison for malicious wounding at the time of his death. I guess the indictment was the straw that broke the camel's back."

"Malicious wounding?" Jennifer said, and then began staring at the empty space between her outstretched hands again.

"I know this all comes as a shock to you, hon," Helen said. "That your father wasn't the saint you thought he was. But it's the truth."

"So what happened? I mean, was there a fight?"

"Not much of one," Helen said. "On the other guy's part I mean.

"We were at the supermarket just before Christmas. Your father and I had picked up a few items and had gotten in the express line to check out, and there was some guy in front of us with thirteen items. I remember your father counting and saying, 'unlucky 13.' The limit was ten I think."

Jennifer listened intently, forgetting the wine for now, though the wine she'd already drunk had not forgotten her. Her head was beginning to spin with the story her mother was telling her.

"He told the guy to get out of line," Helen continued. "The guy looked back, rolled his eyes, and then looked ahead again. That was it. He didn't even say anything. But the next thing I knew, and it happened so fast, your father had this guy on the ground beating the living shit out of him."

"Oh… my… God..." Jennifer whispered.

"The guy almost died, Jennifer. They could have charged your father with attempted manslaughter, but they showed him leniency because of his veteran status."

"Did he ever…" Jennifer could not finish her sentence but her mother knew what she wanted to ask; a mother's intuition.

"He hit me sometimes," she said. "At first, it was completely unintentional."

"How do you *unintentionally* hit someone, mother?"

"In your sleep. Come on, I thought you worked with these guys?

"I'd wake up at times with him wringing my neck. He had the worst nightmares. He'd never tell me what they were about. But once his dreams became physical, at my expense, I started sleeping on the couch."

"I never knew any of this," Jennifer said.

"Of course you didn't. I kept it from you for a reason. You were a baby. But like I said, you're old enough to know now."

"I have no memories of this side of him at all," Jennifer said, almost to herself.

"Because you don't want any, honey. Can't you see that?"

"Repression and denial are powerful," she said, almost whispering, knowing her mother was spot on.

"So you have no recollection of him shaking you nearly to death when you were four years old? On Christmas Eve?" Helen asked.

"What?" Jennifer felt her heart stop, and then a piercing ache in her chest when it started pounding again.

"Yeah," her mother said. "We had just eaten dinner; a ham. And you spilled your father's beer all over the carpet.

"You had grabbed it from the table and were bringing it into the living room for him, trying to be the sweet, daddy's little helper that you always were. You accidentally spilled it and he damn near gave you a seizure he shook you so hard."

At this point, Jennifer felt as if she had lost contact with her body. All the things she'd been told so far were so hard to believe, but *this* was impossible. It had to be.

But she believed it.

She knew her mother had no reason to lie. And it was all so clear to her now, why her mother had never talked about her father. But understanding it and being at peace with it were two different things.

"Oh, he felt so bad about it. He cried with you when he came to and realized what he was doing. He promised never to do it again." She took a long pause before speaking again. "And he never did."

Both sat in silence, Helen reburying the old memories and Jennifer allowing the newly known facts to sink in.

"He finally got you to smile again by throwing you on his lap to pose for a picture. He told you that you always had to smile for the camera, because you always wanted to remember being happy, no matter what.

"It's the picture you always carried around with you when you were growing up. Do you still have it?"

Jennifer wept.

12

Coming home had been bittersweet for Jennifer. She had enjoyed catching up with her mother, but she hadn't enjoyed some of the truths that had finally caught up with her. Her thoughts were swirling now, like debris in the puddles outside, formed from the rain that was now falling all over the greater Seattle area on this mid-Christmas morning.

Maybe I should lighten up a little, she thought. *Think of other things. Get my mind off of it for now.*

She decided to call Rob and wish him a Merry Christmas. She knew that doing so would be in contradiction of the thoughts she'd been having about him and their relationship, but she needed something to get her mind off of her father; anything.

Three rings at his home number found the answering machine working holiday hours. *'Hey you, this is me. Leave a message and I might call you back.'*

That's odd, she thought. It was still early, even back on the east coast, and she didn't imagine he'd be spending time with his children until evening. At least that was how things had always worked out for him on Christmas Day in the past. *Maybe he's on his way to get them?*

She tried his cell, and on the fourth ring she had success.

"Hello?" he said from the other end, nearly three thousand miles away. His voice sounded groggy, tired. Not as if it was filled with the spirit of the season.

"Rob?" she said, thinking perhaps he had a hangover from a bit too much Christmas cheer the night before. Her mother was still in bed here on the west coast sleeping off her hangover.

"Well, Jennifer. How interesting to hear from you."

"Sorry," she said. "I know I've been out of touch for a while. But I wanted to call and wish you a merry Christmas." She paused. "Is everything ok there? Where are you? On your way to get your kids?"

"No," he said. "I'm in the hospital. Merry Christmas to me."

"Hospital. Rob, what happened?"

"Interesting that you should ask," he said, bitter groggy now coming through satellite and space (what would have been 'the line' a generation before). "Some crazy war vet damn near beat me to death the day before yesterday at the DMV!"

Her heart stopped, and she felt as if she were about to hear a sequel to the story her mother had told her about her father the night before. *Bat shit crazy war vet, two; the next generation,* she thought.

"Rob, what…"

"Do you know some psycho named Corey Prine?"

"Wha…" she was speechless. Her tongue and lips were moving but no words were coming out of her mouth. Her mind went into high gear. "I can't tell you whether I do or don't Rob. You know that. But what happened? What does it have to do with this Prine guy?"

"Dude comes in to renew his driver's license," Rob said, his voice less groggy, as if he were either waking up or coming out of any drug induced fog he may have been in. "Claimed he was in Iraq when they expired. Hey, I can believe that. Happens all the time.

"But he'd had a Virginia license, so the state of Virginia was involved. I guess he didn't like hearing what they had to say or something, so he came across the damn counter, like it was my fault.

"I don't even remember it really. I guess he knocked me out quick and early. But thank God for witnesses and security cameras. They saw it all.

"Sum bitch kept beating me even though I was out cold! Hell, they might put him away for attempted manslaughter." He paused long enough to catch his breath. "And they will, by God, if *I* have anything to do with it!"

"Oh my God, Rob, are you ok? I mean, obviously not if you're in the hospital. But what's wrong with you? I mean, what are your injuries? Are you at the VA?"

Rob told her yes, he was in the VA hospital in Beckley, and then he listed all of his injuries, in proper medical terminology, just as his doctors had done for him three dozen times in the past sixty hours.

'Perforated left ear drum. Disconnected retina of the left eye. Disconnected nose cartilage (the nose with the broken bridge). Three broken ribs on left side of rib cage. Fractured tibia.'

And what the doctors hadn't mentioned, but Rob did to Jennifer, one hell of a pounding headache.

"Jesus Christ," she whispered, her words floating on soft air. "Jesus Christ."

"So, do you know the sum bitch?"

"Rob, I can't say if I do or I don't. What's important now isn't whether I know this guy or not, but making sure you're ok. Are you going to be ok?"

"Oh yeah," he said. "Remember, I'm an old soldier myself."

Jennifer tried not to chuckle.

"If I'da known he was comin' for me, I'da put his punk, E-4 ass out like a light."

"How did you know he was an E-4, Rob? How much did you talk to this guy before all this happened?"

"Enough," he said.

"Rob?" she drew the word out the way she had a tendency to do when working with her patients. "Did you do anything to provoke this guy?"

"I knew you'd say that!" he barked into the phone. "You are *always* taking the side of these cry baby whiners! That's the problem with you!"

His reaction instantly reminded her of her previous thoughts on their relationship. Her original line of thinking, that she should not be in a relationship with Rob at all, had just been confirmed.

"Rob," she said. "It's Christmas. Let's not go here." She paused, feeling that he could probably see her in his mind's eye, lowering her head and shaking it with her eyes closed. "I'm sorry that what has happened to you has happened, and that you are where you are. Especially today. But merry Christmas."

"Yeah," he said, a bitter pout. "Some Christmas for me."

"My mom is calling me Rob. I need to go," she lied.

"Your mom's here?"

"No, I'm in Washington."

"Wow," he said, no longer sounding so wrapped up in himself. "I wouldn't have thought you would have gone out there."

"There's a lot about me that you wouldn't have thought."

"What's that mean?"

"I'm not so sure I know myself. But I will." She paused and then said the words again, but this time for herself. "I will."

"What does any of that mean, Jen?"

"Goodbye Rob." She hung up the phone and immediately dialed Corey's home number.

"Hello?" Corey's mother said in a very anxious voice after one ring.

"Mrs. Prine?"

"Yes?"

"This is Jennifer Hutton, Corey's VA counselor. I was just calling some of my vets this morning to wish them a merry Christmas. Is Corey around?"

"Thank God you called," Mrs. Prine said. "Corey's in jail."

13

*Meeting between Jennifer Hutton (L.C.S.W.) and Corey Prine
December 29, 2010

"You didn't have to come back early because I got in trouble," Corey said and then sat down in his regular chair in Jennifer's office.

"I know I didn't *have* to, Corey," she said. "But wouldn't you agree that it was the right thing to do? Regardless of what

you think, someone cares about you. Lots of people care about
you, and I'm one of them; and your parents, and your fellow
vets, and a grateful nation."

"Don't start that grateful nation shit with me Jennifer!
This grateful nation has charged me with malicious wounding, and
wants to send me to prison for two to ten years after already
having sent me to hell for one. *Fuck* this grateful nation!"

"Corey," she said, lowering her tone, but not backing down
in spite of his anger. "You almost killed a man. And why? What
did he do to you?"

"What did he do to me? What did he do to me?" Corey was
leaning forward, his eyes bulging out of his red face, and he
was gripping the arms of the chair so fiercely that Jennifer
thought the cheap, imitation wood they were made out of might
crack. "I don't know what you've heard but I am worthy of a
little respect, even at the D.M.V. And they can see when my
fucking insurance lapses on a truck I don't own any more, but
they can't fucking see when I am in Iraq? And they won't take my
word… no, they won't take a certified copy of my DD-214
(military 'permanent record') for it?"

"Corey," Jennifer said, shutting her eyes and holding up
her hand, showing him the palm. "Calm down. I want you to sit
back in your chair."

He did.

"Start at the beginning, and tell me exactly what happened
at the D.M.V."

This was the story: Two days before Christmas, Corey Prine
walked into the Department of Motor Vehicles office in Beckley,
West Virginia to renew his driver's license which had expired
while he was serving in Iraq.

"I was in the Army myself," the teller he'd spoken to had
said; some guy named Rob. It said so on his name badge.

"That's cool," Corey said. "So which hell hole did you go
to? Iraq or Afghanistan?"

"Oh, I didn't deploy," Rob the teller said. "I got out just after September eleventh."

"Oh," Corey said, very nonchalantly. A little too nonchalantly for Rob the teller's liking.

"I was an E-6," Rob said, his eyebrows furrowing. "E-6 promotable! Had I re-upped I would have been an E-7, platoon leader."

"That's cool man."

"Well, what was your rank?" Rob the teller asked, as Corey took his expired Virginia driver's license out of his wallet.

"I was an E-4, specialist. I served as a machine gunner for a convoy security team in Iraq."

"Oh, so you think that since you deployed and I didn't that you're mister big shot, and I'm not worthy? My rank means nothing?"

"First of all," Corey began, trying to keep his anger in check. "You're not in the Army anymore, so your rank doesn't mean *anything*. Secondly, it sounds as if *you* are the one who has problems with never having deployed, not me." He paused, watching his friendly D.M.V. teller fume. "Now, I'm not here for a dick measuring contest. That's one of the things I *don't* miss about the military. I'm here to renew my license that expired while I was in Iraq."

"Is this clean?" Rob asked, taking Corey's expired license and holding them up to his eyes for close inspection.

"What does that mean?"

"I mean why didn't you take care of this before you deployed? You knew the expiration date was coming up."

"My dad asked me the same question," Corey said, his voice flat and cool. "And I'll tell you the same thing I told him. I was just a little pre-occupied, worrying about getting my legs blown off by a road side bomb, to catch everything here before I deployed. Like my driver's license."

"Yeah," Rob said, sounding as Corey imagined Napoleon Bonaparte might have sounded once getting up on the back of his white mare and then looking down at a man who had previously towered above him. "Now look at you. Now that you're back you have to deal with all this."

"And thank God for that," Corey said.

"What?" Rob asked, crinkling his face in confusion.

"Because that means I made it back. Now can you do this for me, or do I need to talk to your supervisor?"

"Wait here," Rob said before walking to the back office. Corey could see him pounding away on the computer through the large glass window.

Corey had no opinion on the D.M.V. guy's lack of deployment, but he had dealt with his kind before, 'Peace time warriors' they were called. They seemed insecure about never having been deployed, truly tested by fire, and for some reason a good many of them liked to take their insecurities out on those who had. Corey had gotten good at ignoring them and blowing them off.

For a time.

Corey felt a surge of adrenaline when he noticed Rob pick up the phone in the small room on the other side of the glass window. A minute or so of inactivity on Rob's part went by and then he started talking into the phone while holding Corey's driver's license up and to his face like he had before. After a moment, Rob motioned Corey in with the waving of his hand.

"What's going on?" Corey asked.

"Have a seat, specialist," Rob the teller said, as if he were still a squad leader back in the Army and then he put the phone on speaker. "I have him with me here now, and we're all on speaker phone."

"Mr. Prine?" a woman's voice came through from the Virginia end of the call.

"Yes," Corey said.

"I'm Sally Gray from the Virginia Department of Motor Vehicles. How are you today, Sir?"

"Well, I don't know yet," he said. "What's going on with my license?"

"We are showing in our system that the auto insurance on your 2004 Dodge Dakota lapsed last April. As you know, carrying auto insurance in the state of Virginia is required by law. Since you had a lapse we cannot release the hold we've placed on your driver's license until you can show us proof that you renewed your policy. Lack of proof will result in a fine of $600 to release the hold."

"Oh," Corey said with a sigh of relief and a light chuckle. "I thought it was something serious. This isn't a problem. Do you know where I was last April? And why the insurance policy lapsed?"

"No sir, I don't, but if you can explain it to me and provide proof, I'd love to clear this up for you."

"I was in Iraq," Corey said. "And my wife at the time had wrecked the truck, and instead of fixing it with the money she received from the insurance company, she sold the truck and pocketed the money. And that was before the lapse anyway, of course. So the truck was not owned by me at the time the policy lapsed, and I wasn't even in the country."

"This isn't a problem, Mr. Prine," the friendly voice from Virginia said. "Do you have your DD-214 there with you to verify your dates of deployment?"

"I sure do."

"Great. Just pass it over to the gentleman there with you and he can verify it for us, and I'll go ahead and lift the hold for you here in Virginia, and you shouldn't have any further problems getting your license as long as there are no problems in West Virginia."

Corey had already dug the DD-214 out of his manila envelope in which he also had copies of his birth certificate and recent tax returns. He handed it to Rob.

"I hate to rain on everyone's parade here," Rob the teller said, holding the form up to his face just like he had the license earlier. "But we've had some problems with these here recently."

"What are you talking about?" Corey said, feeling his blood pressure begin to rise. He'd assumed the dick measuring contest was over.

"We've had alot of 'ol boys coming in here claiming to have been deployed to Iraq or Afghanistan, and trying to get out of other troubles, like driving on restricted licenses or whatever." Rob was smiling while he talked. "And they've been coming in with some forged DD-214's. Turns out most of 'em never even served."

"What!" Corey said. He wasn't surprised at the story Rob the teller had given, he could believe it, but he was surprised that he would pull this stunt when he could simply verify the authenticity of the form, which he knew was real. Give him, Corey, what he wanted, roll up his measuring tape and put it away, and get on with life.

This guy really had been an N.C.O., Corey thought.

"We've had that happen here, too," the voice from Virginia said. "Rob was it?"

"That's right."

Rob the teller, Corey thought.

"Are you uncomfortable verifying the authenticity of the DD-214 that Mr. Prine has brought to you?"

"I am," he said, and then he smiled even bigger. "I wouldn't be if it just hadn't happened so many times. I don't want to get my ass in a sling if this is another fake."

"You son of a bitch," Corey mumbled. Not loud enough for Sally Gray in Virginia to hear it, but certainly loud enough for Rob the teller to hear it.

"Sorry for this slight inconvenience Mr. Prine," Sally said. "But this problem is easily resolved."

"How is this easily resolved?" Corey said, glaring at Rob as if he wanted to rip his throat out. The smile Rob was giving him wasn't helping.

"We'll just need you to get in touch with your company commander from your deployment, and have him send us a certified letter that you were indeed deployed with his unit during the period in question."

"You are fucking kidding me!"

"I'm sorry Mr. Prine, but we have had too many people taking advantage of the system lately."

"So this government is capable of sending my ass to Iraq, and knowing damn well I'm there while I'm there, 'cause otherwise they'd lock me up in prison for desertion if I wasn't, but then when I get back, you fucktards aren't capable of seeing that I was there when I was there? When it comes to something as simple as renewing my driver's license?"

"I'm sorry, Mr. Prine. That's all I can do. Once you talk to your C.O. just have him send the letter to us at our office here in Richmond. Any of us working here will be able to lift the hold on the system once we get the letter. You can get our address from our website."

Rob the teller thanked Sally Gray from Virginia and hung up the phone and then he looked at Corey Prine and smiled his best shit eating grin from ear to ear.

Corey blacked out.

And then Rob the teller spent Christmas in the hospital.

* * *

"So you don't remember any of what you did after Rob hung up the phone?" Jennifer asked after Corey's precise, extremely accurate review of the events at the D.M.V. from the week before.

"None of it," he said.

"Corey, we have a problem. You're facing up to ten years for something you can't even remember doing."

"I'd say the problem here is that I don't give too much of a fuck."

"What do you mean, Corey? How can you not care about this? It's your freedom we're talking about."

"I spent a year in Iraq, getting abused by my leadership and getting fucked over by anyone who could fuck me over back here. And now that I'm back, I'm still getting fucked over.

"And this time all because some prick with combat envy (*Jennifer made a mental note to remember that terminology for later use*) didn't like it that I didn't blow him because he used to be a staff sergeant. I could do time in a U.S. prison on my fucking head compared to my time in Iraq, and people would be safer with me there anyway, obviously."

"Corey, were you drinking the day you went to the D.M.V.?"

"Hell no!" he said, and he hadn't been. But boy had he tied one on the night before.

"Where you on any drugs other than the ones you've been prescribed through the VA?"

"No!" he said, and again, he hadn't been. But he'd planned on getting baked once he got home on some prime weed he'd bought the day before from the high school girl that lived beside his parents. He was lucky he'd left it at home instead of having taken it with him to the D.M.V., with his little unplanned meeting with law enforcement and all.

"Corey, I want to do something for you. It will certainly help your court case, but more importantly, I hope it will save your life. Or someone else's."

"What?"

"I want to recommend that you go inpatient for a few days."

"What the hell is that?"

"It's nothing to be frightened of," she said, leaning forward and placing her palms flat on her desk. "We'll send you off to our inpatient, psychiatric ward down in Salem, Virginia. You'll get daily therapy, and they can try some different medications and perhaps find one that can keep you from repeating the incident you had before Christmas."

"You want to lock me up?" He was incredulous. "And get me on more drugs? You know, you've gone from being anti-meds to being a goddamn pharmacist!"

Jennifer said nothing for a moment, because she knew that Corey was right. But things had changed. They had changed with Corey of course, but things had also changed with her. After the long talk with her mother, she wasn't quite so sure that all of her previous stances and thoughts on how to treat and deal with vets were the same. She had facts now that she hadn't had before, and she wasn't quite sure what to believe in light of those facts, and she felt that she should explain all of this to Corey so he would understand her sudden three sixty.

"Corey," she said. "I want to share something with you that I have no business sharing with you or anyone."

Corey sat back in his chair. He had always appreciated Jennifer's sincerity and her honesty. In spite of so often being blinded by anger, he knew that she really cared. She wouldn't have flown all the way across the country during the holidays if she didn't.

"I'm listening," he said, and the tone of his voice let her know that she stood a chance of convincing him to voluntarily go inpatient.

She shared with him the real history of her father, as it had recently been told to her by her mother; the fight he had been in when he went into a similar P.T.S.D. blackout; his abuse toward her mother that eventually led to abuse toward her as a little girl. She told him, now that she knew the truth, she no longer held the same views on how, specifically, to help her vets.Her practice was going through a metamorphosis, quickly, and he was the first caterpillar in the cocoon.

"Corey," she said, finishing up, her eyes swelling with tears. "You're just like my daddy. To a 'T.' The fight, the anger. All of it.

"I'm afraid that if we don't take drastic measures, you're going to end up having some kind of accident."

She made quotation signs with the fingers of both of her hands, indicating that the *accident*, if it did come, would not be quite the *accident* it might appear to be.

"I couldn't live with that, and I don't want that for you," she said.

He looked down at his hands in reflection. "You think it will help?" he looked up, tears now swelling in his eyes also.

"I do."

He held his wrists out to her, turned up, with his hands balled into fists. "Let 'em take me away."

Jennifer picked up her phone and called for two orderlies, and then she and Corey cried together.

14

Corey was hardly aware of the four hours he spent sitting in a private room at the VA hospital in Beckley waiting for an ambulance ride to the VA hospital in Salem, Virginia. He could remember a couple of different doctors, at least he thought they had been doctors, coming in and shaking his hand and calling him buddy and thanking him for his service and telling him that everything was going to be ok.

He remembered the ride in the ambulance. It wasn't a long ride, but the prick medic that sat in the back with him and wouldn't shut the hell up sure made it seem long.

"I aint never served but I got all kinds'a rah'spect for those of ya'll that have," he'd kept saying. That and stuff like, "Man, I bet you seen lots'a shit. 'Cause you're quiet. The one's that run they mouths all the time are lying and didn't see shit. Man, I bet you seen lots'a shit. Cause you're quiet."

The medic spit snuff juice into an empty Go-Mart big gulp cup after every comment.

Corey had tried shutting his eyes to act as if he were sleeping. It worked for a little while, because Corey could sense the guy slide up into the shotgun position of the meat wagon, but the guy must have been keeping an eye on him because when he opened his eyes the guy came sliding back to the rear of the ambulance again.

"Man, I wasa-readin' your file," he said when he started again, with what he obviously thought was praise. "You got that combat action badge. Man, I bet you seen lots'a shit."

Corey had not particularly been looking forward to getting locked up on a psych ward, but when they finally got to the hospital in Salem, he was glad that they had. *Anything to get away from the real psycho in the back of the ambulance,* he thought.

He hadn't known what to expect as he was walked to 'the ward' as they called it, but he had his guard up, as he had when he had walked into the regional jail in central West Virginia the week before.

A very loud, middle aged black man approached Corey as soon as he was seated in the waiting area of the ward. Corey thought the guy sounded as if he were talking with shit in his mouth.

"Whah-yo in-fo-mah?" he had said.

"Leave him alone and go back to your assigned seat, Herman," an aid had said, coming over quickly to save Corey from having to have a conversation with such an interesting character.

"Wha owe fo blah Je-uh yo!" Herman said as he was being pulled away.

What the fuck? Corey thought. *Did he say black Jesus?*

"Mr. Prine?"

The voice had come from behind Corey. He turned to see a middle-aged white man with a tie and very little hair over a shiny scalp motion him into the room the man was half sticking out of. *This*, Corey thought, *must be the shrink.*

"How are you doing today, Mr. Prine?" the man said, motioning Corey to sit in the chair across from his desk. "My name is Byron Blevins. I'm the head social worker on the ward here." He began leafing through Corey's file in front of him. "Oh, I see you are from West Virginia?"

"Yes," Corey said, feeling as if he were about to be engrossed with more head shrink bullshit. "Hinton."

"I used to live in Summersville. I was a social worker for Nicholas County. Have you been there?"

"I've passed through," Corey said. "On my way to go fishing on the Cranberry over in Richwood."

"Oh yes," Byron said. "Richwood. Nice place. I worked with a guy that lives on top of a mountain over there. Fork Mountain, I think it is."

"Never heard of it," Corey said.

"Oh well," Blevins said. "It's neither here nor there." He paused, reflecting on the past; the man on Fork Mountain and Fork Mountain itself. "I always got some strange vibes up there though."

Corey cleared his throat in a *'what the fuck'* kind of way.

"Sorry," Blevins said. "So, I understand from talking to Jennifer Hutton in Beckley that you've had some recent problems with the law?" He raised his eyebrows for confirmation.

"Yep," Corey said.

"And Jennifer feels this was due to anger associated with P.T.S.D., and that you may have even been in a P.T.S.D. induced black out?"

"That's what she told me," Corey said.

"Ok," Blevins said. "You are in a safe place here, first of all. There are no threats to you."

Corey rolled his eyes then began studying the walls. There were so many framed degrees and licenses hanging all over them. Corey could tell that if nothing else, the guy across the desk from him had spent a lot of time in classrooms. Maybe he knew what he was talking about?

"… ignore that if you hear it. It doesn't really pertain to you."

"I'm sorry, what?" Corey said, busted paying no attention.

"Black Jesus," Blevins said. "You'll hear alot of these guys talking about Black Jesus. Don't listen to them. That's something that doesn't pertain to you."

"Yeah," Corey said, sitting up in his chair with interest. "Some black dude out there was mumbling something about what sounded like 'black Jesus.'"

"Oh, that's Herman. Especially stay away from him."

"Is he dangerous?"

"No," Blevins said, looking down and shaking his head. "He's perfectly harmless. And perfectly sane."

"What?"

"I shouldn't tell you this, Corey. Is it ok if I call you Corey? You seem too young to go by Mr. Prine."

Corey said it was ok to call him Corey and then Blevins leaned over his desk a little as if he were going to tell him a grave secret.

"Most of the people on the ward, most meaning all really, have nothing wrong with them."

"Then why are they here?" Corey asked.

"They are doing, what you call, milking the system. They're here to try to get a check from the government one way or the other. They've been denied by either the VA or social security, or both, and they know that spending *any* amount of time locked up on the ward is a sure fire way to start getting a check.

"You are actually the only one here now who has deployed to a combat zone. Most of these guys served a couple years in the Army Reserves or National Guard during peace time. Maybe the Navy."

"That's disgusting!" Corey said, anger apparent by the look on his face.

"It is," Blevins agreed. "But at some time, they did serve, so they are as entitled to the services of the VA as any of you who have deployed. So, I'm telling you this because I respect where you've been and what you've done, and I don't want you to let any of them get under your skin, or pull you into their little fantasy worlds with their war stories that never happened." Blevins paused and then said, "And these are the guys who make it so hard for those of you who are really suffering to get the help you need. They've turned a system that is supposed to help you into a watch dog group that ends up biting you so badly."

"Well, I appreciate that," Corey said. "But what's up with this *black Jesus* stuff?"

"That," Blevins said, and then leaned back in his chair and looked around the room as if to make sure there was no one else in it. "There's somewhat of an 'urban legend' associated with this ward; Black Jesus.

"Supposedly, he visits some of the patients while they are here. Always at night. And he somehow changes them. When they leave, if they've seen 'black Jesus,' they get one hundred percent approval from both the VA and social security. And somehow," he continued, hesitantly, "Once they've *seen* this *black Jesus,* they *do* actually have all the injuries and symptoms that allow them to completely qualify for the benefits. No questions asked."

"What?" Corey asked, utterly confused.

"I can assure you that this *black Jesus* is not real," Blevins said. "And you have nothing to worry about in regard to the legend. Anyone who has ever made these claims has been the type of person that comes in here for a check and has never been deployed. I'm not sure how the thing works specifically, or why, but I can tell you, that anyone who has actually deployed has *never* seen black Jesus, or even claimed to."

"Ok," Corey said. "I understand." But he had never been more confused in his life.

15

*Meeting between Jennifer Hutton (L.C.S.W.) and Jerry Barnes, Ph.D., Ed.d. former M.D.- December 30, 2009

"So how was Washington, my dear?" Dr. Barnes asked as Jennifer sat in the overstuffed chair that she thought she was getting a little too used to. She noticed that there was a fire burning in the small fireplace to her left. Until now she had thought the fireplace was only ornamental. She found both the warmth of the fire and the radiance of the flames comforting.

"Very eye opening," she said. "You were right. It was worth the trip, and I learned more about the realities of my father than I could have imagined."

"Do tell, Jennifer. I'm up for a dance. Shall I grab some leftover mistletoe?"

Dr. Barnes relaxed in his wheelchair, his arthritic fingers nestling the oxygen tube dangling from his nose while he listened to Jennifer's recap of the conversation she'd had with her mother in which it was revealed to her that her father had not been the knight in shining armor she had thought, but rather a very deranged Vietnam vet that she may be all the better off for not having been raised by.

"Things are not always as they appear," he said after she finished. "How is this affecting you in your work? As far as how you view what you do, and how you do it?"

"It has utterly confused me," she said.

"How so?"

"Everything I thought I knew just isn't so," she said. "I had so many beliefs, and they were all based on an artificial reality."

"Ah," Dr. Barnes said. "Tastes just like culture shock, doesn't it?"

"What?" her eyebrows furrowed. Dr. Barnes was always throwing sidesteps into his 'dances' and they were always of the most curious design.

"Culture shock," he said. "All culture is, is a belief system passed down from generation to generation, usually started out of necessity for survival within a race, or a certain region. Often times, these ways of living become obsolete, but we keep them anyway.

"For instance, it is considered rude to stare in American culture. Some even perceive it as a slight, or a direct threat. Why, many men have fought it out and even been killed over a stare down.

"In some of our cities, there are ordinances against staring and fines for doing so for this very reason."

"I did not know that," Jennifer said, raising her eyebrows at this interesting yet so far seemingly needless lesson. She'd store the information away, she thought, in the event she was ever on Jeopardy.

"It comes from the old days of the great American southwest," he said. "The time when everyone was trying to establish themselves as King Billy Badass of the nether regions, and if you wanted to shoot it out with someone who thought he was the king? Why, stare him down. A duel would come.

"And in our society, staring has been viewed, ever since, as a threat or a challenge. Even though we left the days of the wild,wild west behind more than a hundred and fifty years ago."

"Right," she said, still curious to the relevancy of his little history lesson.

"In most Eastern cultures, it is considered a compliment to be stared at. It means that the person staring at you finds you very attractive."

"What do you mean?" she said. "What does this have to do with my situation?"

"Do you know how many Vietnamese civilians were gunned down and slaughtered because of the simple misunderstanding of the stare down during Vietnam? Or the same for the Koreans during the Korean War?"

"Oh," she said, understanding dawning."

"When we don't know the facts, or the relevancy behind the facts, people can die, Jennifer. Those soldiers in Asia, always in fear for their lives, knew that on any given day they could be gunned down or grenaded by anyone. It would have never crossed their minds that all those peasants in those third world villages were staring at them so intently because they found them attractive. Another fact about Asian culture, they've always found light skinned people attractive, and it all has to do with socioeconomics.

"If you were of light complexion, for thousands of years in Asia and throughout the Middle East, it was because you were wealthy and spent most of your time indoors, and avoided the blazing sun. You had servants out in the sun tending to your crops. And if you were dark, well, you were one of the servants. You were of the lower class, and of course, deemed as less attractive.

"But anyway, our G.I.'s in all the wars in Asia simply saw serious looks coming from serious looking faces, the face of the enemy in their U.S. Government spoon-fed minds, and often they would open fire and wipe out entire villages. And they thought they were doing it for their own protection, because the fact was, they were being stared at.

"But the fact behind the fact is that it was because they were all just so goddamn handsome." He threw his head back with a chuckle. "More than fifty thousand Vietnamese it is estimated died for staring during the Vietnam conflict."

Then Jennifer said, "And I've held certain beliefs in my practice, and I've been treating my vets in certain ways, because of the beliefs I've held about my father and his death."

"Yes," Dr. Barnes concurred. "And what you've been doing could end up being just as fatal to someone as the stares directed toward westerners in the Far East." He paused, giving his words time to sink in before speaking again. "So how is your thinking different after your little trip to the west coast?"

"I know my father didn't die in any accident," she said, without even taking the time to consider her answer.

"So you *do* believe now that your father committed suicide? Rather than that he simply died in a single vehicle, albeit a tractor trailer, accident?"

"Yes," she said.

"And how might you have done things differently for your father, had you been treating him? Or, how might you do things differently today with a man like your father?"

"Interesting that you should ask," she said and then leaned forward in her chair. "I've talked to you about a patient of mine in the past. Corey Prine?"

"Yes," Dr. Barnes said. "I remember him being a very angry young man; a ticking time bomb. The one who fears there may be no *off switch* for his condition."

"Yes," she said.

"And how is our young Mr. Prine doing now?"

"He's currently locked up on *the ward* down in Salem."

"Oh?" Dr. Barnes raised an eyebrow. "And what has happened with Mr. Prine, to cause his incarceration? I mean institutionalization?"

Jennifer told Dr. Barnes about the fight before Christmas at the DMV. She conveniently neglected to tell him that Corey's victim had been the man with whom she had been sharing a bed with whenever her hormones had convinced her to do so for the past several years. And she even more conveniently neglected to mention that part of her was more than a little smug that Rob had gotten his ass royally kicked by one of her so called "whiners" as Rob himself referred to her patients.

"You know what will happen at Salem, don't you, Jen?" Dr. Barnes asked, and like any good lawyer (*fucking* lawyers- as he would say) he already knew the answer to his own question.

"Yes," she said. "They'll try some new meds. Maybe find the right mix."

"They will certainly try new meds. Why, they have all those contracts with those large pharmaceutical companies they have to satisfy. But Jen, come now. You really don't think they'll find a combo that works, do you, dear?"

"I don't know," she said, leaning back into her chair and sighing. "I really hope they do."

"Before, you never believed in meds, did you?"

"No," she said in a voice that sounded half defeated. "But like I said, after finding out the truth about my dad, I think differently.

"You asked what I would do if I had been able to treat him. I would have done the same for him. I would have had him placed into inpatient care, hoping they'd find the right mix."

"The key word you keep using, Jen, is 'hope.' I think you know in your heart what the truth is."

Jennifer sat in silence. Sometimes she hated that Dr. Barnes was always right.

"Why, our young Mr. Prine has pointed it out himself. *There is no off switch*. And that would *include* any 'proper mix' of U.S. Government engineered and backed dope they are pushing out to tens of thousands of these guys through the VA."

"I know," she said, merely a whisper. "I know."

"So now, dear," he said, rolling toward her in his wheelchair and taking both of her hands in his. "Now is the time that you are really to be tested by fire. When you face your own truths you've neglected. Truths that change the fundamental beliefs in everything you thought you knew before; truths that will change you at your core.

"You can quit or you can proceed. But you must proceed with caution, because from here, everything changes entirely. Are you ready to learn a new dance?"

"I don't know," she said. "I really don't know."

16

"Mind if I sit here?" Corey asked.

The woman he'd addressed, who he thought appeared to be in her early thirties, looked scared to death. She was sitting all alone in a wrinkled bathrobe at a table off to the side of the small dining room on the ward. Her back was against the wall.

"Are you safe?" she said, looking up at him with calculating eyes.

"I am if you are," he said, and then he looked around nervously, a quick glance left, followed by a quick glance to the right.

"Go ahead," she said and then motioned to the chair across the table from her with a nod. "You just get here today?" she asked, and then she shoveled a spoonful of gruel into her mouth.

"Yeah," Corey said, inspecting the gruel on his tray with his spork, as if it were an earthworm he was getting ready to dissect in science class. He remembered that when he *had* done so way back in high school, his science teacher had gotten the class's attention before the dissection began by eating a worm. Corey had thought it was gross at the time, as had all the other students, but at this moment, he was thinking that he'd gladly trade his tray of gruel for a plate of earth worms. "How long you been here?"

"About a week," she said, shoveling another mouthful of gruel as she spoke. "Don't worry, you'll be able to eat it in a couple days," she said after reading the look that was on his face while he gazed at his food. "My name's Heather."

"You get used to it, huh? I'm Corey."

"Hell no," she said. "You just get so damn hungry, and there are no other options."

"Oh," he said, making a lateral incision.

"So, you okay?" she asked, nervously glancing left to right, keeping her eyes on the other patients.

"Yeah," he said. "Just went a little crazy last week. Beat the shit out of some asshole."

"Well, you know what Norman Bates says in the movie *Psycho*, right?"

Corey looked up, confused. He told her that, no, he didn't know what Norman Bates said in the movie *Psycho*.

"It's ok," she said, quoting. "We all go a little crazy sometimes."

"You're right there," Corey said and then chuckled. He tried a taste of the gruel and then quickly returned the spork and the uneaten portion of gruel to his tray. "Guess I'll have to wait till my body starts digesting itself. So why you here?"

"I come about twice a year," she said. "When I get a little stressed and burned out."

"Oh?" Corey said. "From what, life?"

"I work for the VA" Heather said. "And dealing with the whole ball of mess makes me go crazy and blow my stack about every six months. So I come here to recharge the old battery, then outward and onward I go."

"Which VA?" Corey asked, drawing a heart into the gruel on his tray and then cutting it out with the spork.

"I'd rather not say," she said. "I'm in administration."

Corey respected her privacy and didn't push it.

"I make too much money to quit ya know," she said. "Wouldn't want to anyway. I really love what I do, but man does it get stressful."

"I couldn't imagine," he said.

"Oh, it's terrible," she said. "You guys, well," she hesitated, looking around the room at the other patients, and then she asked him if he had deployed. He told her that, yes, he had deployed; to Iraq.

"Some of you guys do so much for all of us," she said. "Then you come home and you have to wait around forever to get the help you need. And some of you never get it."

"Delay, deny and hope that I die," Corey said.

"Exactly," she said. "And the sad fact about that little saying is that it isn't a joke. It's real. I've seen it in action and have had it ordered down to me from the top."

"No way," he said, looking up to meet her eyes.

"You have no clue," she said. "Do you know how much money the VA saves every time a vet commits suicide?"

"What?" he said, a hint of incredulity in his voice. "A grand a month, maybe? How much is *that* in the grand scheme of things?"

"A grand a month, times twelve months in a year, times sixty years in the case of some of these kids coming back from the war," she said. "Do the math. It adds up to quite a chunk. More than a million dollars per vet just in disability pay even if it is only a grand a month.

"Now, add to that, the costs of their medical care. Now you've just quad-tripled the amount. Until they get old. Then you've multiplied it innumerable times because they need so much more healthcare when they're old."

"Wow," Corey said, astonished. "I never thought of it in those terms."

"Of course not," she said. "You've been distracted with putting your life back together. If you want to see the proof in the pudding, just Google the topic of VA compensation for ailments pertaining to Agent Orange exposure from the Vietnam

War. You'll see that the benefits go up every twelve to twenty four months.

"They already know all the problems it has caused the vets who were exposed to it forty to fifty years ago. They knew about it at the time. But they knew the costs also, so they let them die off in batches of ten thousand to twenty thousand each before releasing more parts of the information, piecemeal, and especially before releasing the new benefits. It would break the bank otherwise. Keep Googling it every year or so for shits and giggles. You'll see.

"And the same thing is going to happen to your generation of veterans in regard to the waves sent out by those juke systems, the things you guys used over there to block the cell phone frequencies to keep the roadside bombs from blowing up on you as much as they did when you went by.

"Now," she said, her eyes getting big, as if she had told a game show host from one of those weekday game shows from her childhood that she would take what was behind door number three, though she felt as if she were the host, and she was getting ready to show *Corey* what was behind door number three. "Multiply all those numbers by the amount of vets offing themselves, and you see how much the government is saving in the long run. As of now, a vet from the oil wars, the wars in the Middle East they're calling them, is attempting suicide every eighty minutes. And there are people within the U.S. Government that want to see that rate double!"

"What!" Now Corey *was* incredulous. No hint about it.

"Oh, but when I start going crazy about this kinda stuff, they send me here to shut me up. They could fire me, but I know a little too much about a few too many people."

"Like what? And who?"

"Like my boss to start with. And how his dick tastes."

"What!" Corey sat up straight now, quickly. One of the orderlies looked over and took a half step in their table's direction before relaxing.

"Yeah," she said and then giggled. "Moment of weakness. We were at a party a few years ago, and he gave me a ride home afterward. I gave *him* a ride when he came in my apartment.

"It never happened again. But hey, he's married, and was at the time. I'm not and wasn't then either. So I guess you can call it job security, huh?"

"That's crazy," Corey said. "But yeah, I guess."

They sat in a moment of silence while Heather ate more of her gruel and Corey played with his. "It's not like I'd be able to find another job anyway," she said. "Have you been paying attention to this economy?"

"Oh yeah," Corey said. "I haven't been able to find work since I've gotten back."

"Let me guess, you're still in the guards or reserves."

"Yes," he said. "The guards for two more years."

"That shit pisses me off," she said. "It makes me sick, all these people in the private sector claiming to support the troops, but won't hire guardsmen or reservists in fear that they might deploy and they'd have to hold their jobs for them.

"When the guys came home from World War Two private industry went out of their way to create jobs for them. As they should have. But now? Good luck getting a job if you haven't E.T.S.'d (exit time in service) yet.

"Could you imagine if soldiers took the same attitude toward the private sector? Just put their weapons down and walked away?"

At that moment, one of the other patients sitting on the opposite side of the room broke into a rap.

"Nigga, nigga, nigga, gonna pull my trigga! Nigga, nigga, nigga, gonna pull my trigga!"

He was a white man, approximately thirty years old. His hair was about two weeks past need of a cut and had a bare streak shaven though it the length of his head, just right of center. His face bore a full beard, except for the bald swatch shaved similarly to the one on his head that started just beside the left of his mouth, traveled down and across his chin, and then down the right side of his neck.

"You race-ah mah fah!" Harold yelled from his seat on the opposite side of the room, gruel falling out of his mouth.

"What the hell is that all about?" Corey asked Heather as they watched an orderly go to the man rapping and then attempt to distract him. The orderly was a plump lady nearing retirement age, and she asked the indie-entertainer if he'd like some ginger ale. She seemed to be as sedated as most of the patients.

"His name's Jeff," Heather said. "Claims to be a record producer or something. He asked me for a blowjob my first day here."

"Wow," Corey said. "Great introduction line."

"Yeah, and as you can tell I'm quite the minority here."

She was right. Corey looked around and saw that she was the only woman on the ward, other than the plump orderly.

"Here's my advice," Heather said, leaning over the table to speak in confidence. "You *can* get some help here. It's not all bullshit.

"Sign up for every group activity they have. They keep a record of your participation in group settings. The more you participate, the quicker you get out."

"Ok," Corey said, listening intently.

"Eat that shit on your tray," she said, pointing at his gruel. "They record that too." She hinted to the table next to them with a nod. Corey looked over and saw that an orderly was leaning over the backs of the patients sitting there and making notations on his pad. "The sooner you learn to eat it, all of it, the quicker you get out."

"Anything else?"

"Participate in all your counseling sessions. Don't just sit there. Ask questions and act interested. Do you get Blevins?"

"Yeah. I guess so I mean. I just met with him."

"Great," she said. "He's easy. Just ask him anything about himself and he'll go on and on for the whole hour. Dude is a fucking flake."

"Ok," he said, making mental note.

"Oh, one more thing."

"What's that?"

"Don't take any meds if they don't explain to you what they are. Especially one they may refer to as a *mood stabilizer*."

"What's that?" Corey asked.

"Hell, even the doctors here don't know. They're always testing these things out on vets and soldiers. You know about all the contracts the D.O.D. and the V.A. has with the big pharmaceutical companies of the world, don't you?"

"Oh yeah," he said. "I was so drugged up in Iraq I didn't think I was *ever* gonna come down. They've been putting me on quite a few pills at the VA already since I've been back."

"Well, you don't want some of the pills they have here. They're using us as guinea pigs, but you don't have to let them. It's your right to decline any meds you don't want to take."

"Ok, thanks," he said.

A middle aged woman, excessively thin and with a head of short, peppered hair rolled a television and a set of speakers on a cart into the dining room. "Time for Karaoke!" she said.

"You have *got* to be fucking kidding me," Corey said to Heather.

"Oh, there's bingo night too," she said. "And remember. If you want out, you need to participate."

"Who's first?" the karaoke lady asked. The room remained silent, other than for a few mumbling sounds coming from a few deeply drugged patients who were conversing with themselves in their own language.

"Got any Garth Brooks?" Corey said, rising to his feet and moving forward, taking what he hoped was his first step back out of here and off of 'the ward.'

17

Dr. Barnes rolled his wheelchair back to his desk and opened the thin drawer in the center. He took out a small key and then leaned over and unlocked the large drawer on the bottom right. He pulled out a large photo album and placed it on his lap and then rolled back to Jennifer.

"Do you remember why I lost my license, dear?"

"Of course, the fucking lawyers," she said and smiled, knowing he'd like her use of his favorite reference for legal professionals. She was right because he smiled also.

"Yes," he said, "because of the fucking lawyers. And the crazy, hopeless vet I'd been working with for a very short period of time who decided to jump off of the New River Gorge one cold, wintry night."

She nodded confirmation of her awareness of the events.

"Do you believe that this man who took a dive was the first veteran I ever worked with who ended up committing suicide, Jennifer?"

"No," she said. "He couldn't have been. You've worked with so many of them over so many years."

"Yes," he said. "I was working with U.S. Government engineered psychos before you were born. And you're right. He *wasn't* the first among the ones I worked with to commit suicide." He looked down, petting the unopened photo album as if it were a cat napping on his lap.

"But I have a confession to make, dear." He looked up and met her eyes. "A confession I've never made to anyone before. And if I couldn't feel my own coffin building itself around me at this very moment (he tugged at the oxygen hose coming out of his nose with his right hand for effect) I probably would not be confessing this to you now."

"You know you can trust me with anything," she said, and he knew that he could.

"That man was not the first vet I ever worked with to commit suicide," he said, "but he *was* the first one who ever committed suicide without my orders to do so."

There was silence.

"I don't understand," Jennifer said. "You didn't tell him not to commit suicide?"

"No, dear," he said, closing his eyes and drawing the corners of his mouth upward, though it wasn't a smile. "I didn't tell *him* to commit suicide."

They sat in silence again, and Dr. Barnes saw the understanding register on Jennifer's face after a few seconds. Her eyes grew wide and her mouth gaped slightly.

"You mean…" she trailed off.

"Yes, dear, I mean I convinced some of my patients to commit suicide."

"But, but…" she said, sounding as she had on the night she'd talked with her mother about her father less than a week before.

"Listen, honey," he said, letting go of the air hose his hand had been lingering on and going back to petting the book in his lap. "Those who treat alcoholics have a saying. And it's a good one. 'Once you've turned a cucumber into a pickle, it can never become a cucumber again.'"

"But how could… we are supposed to…" She was holding her hands up, viewing the invisible objects between them again.

"We have to think of everyone involved, Jen," he said. "We have to think about spouses, children, parents, and society as a whole."

"Yes," she said. "And involve them in the healing process."

"And protect their lives as much as we are trying to protect the lives of our vets, Jen. And sometimes we can only help one of the two sides involved, but not both. And that might sometimes mean eliminating one of the two."

She sat silent, not because she no longer understood, but because she understand too well.

"Reginald Jones," he said, opening the book and turning it to face Jennifer. She looked down and read the headline aloud: 'Vet Found Dead in Apartment Surrounded by Small Arsenal.'

"This guy was pickled, so to say," Dr. Barnes said. "And I don't mean as in drunk. He didn't even drink.

"He had been arrested and incarcerated for assault and battery and domestic violence and public indecency on several occassions."

"Public indecency?" she asked.

"He used to go into Asian restaurants and piss in the buffets."

"Oh," she said.

"Anyway, I could tell it was just a matter of time before this guy did a little more than break a stranger's nose or piss in someone's sum dum cum," he said, chuckling at this last, and Jennifer was amazed that even during his deepest, darkest confessions he could maintain his 'dirty old man' image.

"But even I couldn't have imagined he had plans as grand as he did," Dr. Barnes continued. "They found three dozen guns and more than five thousand rounds of ammo in his house, and maps and blue prints of every military recruiter's office on the eastern seaboard. He was planning one hell of a spree."

"Did you have any idea of what he was up to?" Jennifer asked, her awe in knowing her mentor had been a predecessor to Jack Kevorkian now switching over to the plans behind the man he'd psychologically euthanized.

"No," he said. "But I knew he was up to something, and that time was limited. He'd been in and out of nearly every VA ward on the east coast, and nothing was working; none of the meds nor any of the counseling sessions.

"This guy had left here a cucumber and came back from war a pickle, and there simply was nothing to be done for him, except for locking him up in a padded cell for the rest of his natural days, and it was coming to that quickly. And I didn't want that for him any more than I'm sure you would want it for any of your vets. That is no life, and death is better."

"So how did you get him to do it?" she asked, feeling her stomach turn at the morbidity of the question.

"I simply told him the truth. I said, 'Reggie, I know nothing good is going to come of our sessions, and I know that

you are eventually going to kill someone or many. I know that
you know what is eventually going to happen to you. You are
going to end up going to prison and sharing some cell with some
wild animal, and you will never see daylight again, and you will
just continue to be abused by a system that is broken. But you
will be the one who pays. Now, you can accept that, or you can
follow my advice.'"

"And you advised him to kill himself?" she said.

"You'd better fucking believe I did!"

He leaned forward so forcefully that he almost fell out of
his wheelchair when he spoke. Jennifer instinctively moved
forward, her hands out in front of her to catch him.

"I advised him to go home and stick the business end of
whatever gun he could get his hands on into his mouth and blow
his fucking brains out before the machine could grind him up any
more than it already had." He leaned back into his chair. "Had I
known he'd had such a collection, I would have told him to use
the .44. Turns out he used a .38. Less mess to clean up though,
I guess," he said and then shrugged.

"Wow," Jennifer said. "All the truths I'm finding out this
holiday season."

"Merry Christmas, dear," he said, and then he flipped to
the next page in the album. "Meet Frank Harris."

Jennifer saw the obituary pasted in the book.

"Wife and child beater. Put his twelve year old son in the
hospital for six months for slamming his bedroom door too
loudly," he said. "He ate a bullet before the boy was well."

"And you told him to?" she asked.

"You're fucking right I told him to." He flipped the page
again. "Lucinda Stephens," he said. Jennifer saw the middle aged
woman's faded picture in the aged and yellowed news article, the
headline reading 'Vietnam Medal Winner Found Dead of
Asphyxiation.'

"She had been a nurse in Vietnam," he said. "She confided in me that she would put guys out of their misery if she knew they were too far gone. And trust me, dear. She wasn't the only one over there doing it. Her problem was that she couldn't *stop* doing it once she got home, and she was ending the lives of people who were not miserable and weren't dying."

"You mean," Jennifer said, eyes wide and mouth gaping.

"Yes, dear. She was a serial killer. I tried to get her to O.D. but she was afraid she'd get caught smuggling meds from the hospital where she worked before she was able to get enough out to do it right. So she parked in her garage with the car running on a full tank of gas, and with a hose connected from the tail pipe and running through the window. She took a bottle of Jack, a bag of sour cream and onion potato chips and her cat with her. She went to sleep and never woke up.

"We're up to 1983 now," he continued. "Paul Brewster came later that year," he said, flipping to the next page and next picture. "Then Steven Marlow in '85." He flipped the page again. "Roy Rose in '87."

"I get it," she said, putting her hand on the center of the album so he would stop turning the pages.

"Do you, dear? Are you sure you've learned the dance?"

"I get it," she said.

"But will you be able to do it? When the time is right?"

She stared at him, not with disgust or even disbelief, but in such a way that let him know that she did not know the answer to his question, because she didn't.

"Which is worse to lose, Jennifer, one life or perhaps dozens? Not only do we need to concern ourselves with our vets, but we also need to be concerned about all the other people they interact with, Jen. Do we lose one guy who's pickled beyond repair, or do we watch his entire family or perhaps perfect strangers pay the price and disappear?"

After a moment of silence, Jennifer rose and walked to the bay window. Dr. Barnes' lovely assistants, Anna and Mina, were in the back yard putting away snow shovels. "I certainly have lots to think about," she said when she finally spoke.

"Too much truth at one time can be painful," he said, rolling up behind her. "But you can never have too much of it, and you can never get it too soon."

Jennifer bid him a proper and warm farewell and then went out into the snow, her mind filled with doubt and confusion and feelings she'd never felt.

Dr. Barnes rolled to the front of the fire place and began flipping through the old scrap book again.

Jimmy Crawford, 1989; wife beater and child abuser. He had jumped from the top of the Charleston Civic Center after a 'Poison' Concert.

John Mitchel, 1991, who, during a Vietnam flashback and PTSD blackout while watching news of 'Desert Storm' on CBS, beat his wife into a comma and then killed the family dog.

Then ate it.

He had eaten a bullet from a .243 deer rifle that fall, two days before his first court appearance for domestic violence.

Dr. Barnes felt the pain in his chest again that had visited the last time he had his 'little black book of secrets' out for viewing. He tossed the book into the fire in front of him and grabbed his chest with one hand and his oxygen tube with the other.

As the pages came ablaze, the fire licking its way from the edges of the book to the top of the fireplace, they flipped slowing, methodically, and in order, one by one. As if the hand of the devil were turning them, so that Jerry Barnes could get one last look at his former patients, and be reminded of his former deeds.

There was Peter Smallwood, 1996, who had secretly murdered eight hunters in the woods throughout the mountain state over a fifteen year period with his bow and arrows and his high powered rifles while he had been in the woods hunting.

Hunting people.

Finally, upon Dr. Barnes' convincing, *he* was the one who went into the woods one fine, fall day and didn't return, until a week later, and in a body bag carried out by the fine members of the West Virginia Army National Guard.

As Dr. Barnes watched the pages flip, convinced at one point that he did *indeed* see the devil's hand turning them, his chest pain intensified. He made an attempt to roll to the door to yell for help, but only mentally. His body would not respond to the signals his brain was trying to send it. His left arm remained locked over his chest and his right hand on his oxygen tube.

An hour later, Mina and Anna came into his office for approval of their cute little Ms. New Year outfits he'd wanted them to wear on New Year's Eve. They found him half slumping from his chair, dead, with his feet covered in ashes that had drifted out of the fire place.

They looked at each other as if neither of them knew what to do, shrugging their shoulders, and then left the room. They would call 911, but only after changing back into their regular nurse's assistant's attire. They did not want to be implicated in any way in the dirty old man's death.

18

Corey had taken Heather's advice and warnings to heart, and he was glad he had, because after he sang 'Friend's in Low Places,' and not too far off key, the orderlies came around with their trays of 'skittles.'

"Time to take your skittles, kiddies," they'd said, dancing around like pixie fairies from *Peter Pan*. If it hadn't been for their uniforms, Corey would not have been able to tell them apart from the patients.

"What's this one," Corey had asked when he was handed his cup of 'skittles.'

"Vitamin B-12," was the reply from the thin, middle aged man with a crazed look in his eyes, and a smile that seemed to be painted on like the Joker's. He was missing one of his front teeth, and Corey thought that maybe the guy was on some sort of work release program.

"Have you been dipping into the stash yourself?" Corey asked, placing the pill on the back of his tongue and then chasing it down his throat with water. The insane joker man just stood there, speechless, looking crazy and smiling.

"What's this one?" Corey asked, taking out the next pill.

"That is your Tramadol," the Joker said. "And your Citalopram is in here and some more vitamins."

Corey swallowed the pills he could identify, but when he came to the last one, a salmon colored pill shaped like a football and about the size of a lime seed, he hesitated and asked the Joker what it was.

"Oh, that's just a mood stabilizer," the Joker said.

"No thank you," Corey said, and then he dropped the pill back into the little plastic cup.

"But it will make you feel better," the Joker said, looking crazed, and like he was speaking from experience.

"I know my rights, and I aint takin' it," Corey said. His hillbilly roots and vocabulary always seemed to come out in his speech when he stood his ground. The Joker knew Corey was correct, and had heard the tone in his voice from enough other patients to know not to push the issue if he wanted to keep his other teeth.

The Joker took his little 'mood stabilizer' and his big *Insane Clown Posse* grin and followed the rest of the orderlies out of the room, probably back to Never- Never Land, Corey thought.

An hour later all the patients were ushered to their rooms for lights out. Corey had a private room, though there was an empty bed on the other side for another patient in the event another was to come later.

Corey fell asleep quickly, taxed from the day's dealings with the asshole in the ambulance, listening to Byron Blevins ramble on and on, being briefed by Heather, and then belting his lungs out to some Garth before eating his 'skittles,' which had actually tasted much better than the gruel he had attempted to eat for dinner.

At some point in the middle of the night, and Corey could not tell if he was awake or dreaming when it happened, his door opened. He looked up and saw the Joker coming into his room.

It *had* to be a dream, because this time the Joker had makeup on his face.

And he had that salmon colored pill.

"Just take this and go back to sleep," the Joker said. "This is just a dream anyway. What's it gonna hurt?"

"Okay," Corey said and then did as the Joker had said. He lay back down and then watched as the Joker turned and left the room. He looked back from the door just before he exited, and this time there was no makeup, just that insane look in his eyes and the grin on his face.

Corey realized it was *not* a dream. He was awake and he had taken the 'mood stabilizer.'

"Oh shit!" he said and then popped his head back on his pillow. "This should be interesting."

* * *

"Hellooooo……"

"Hellooooo……"

"Is iiiiiiiiineeeeeeewuuuuunhooooome?"

Corey heard the voice but he couldn't tell where it was coming from, and he didn't know where he was. He saw before him a table, the top of which radiated like the heat waves over a hot highway in summer. He looked up a little and could see a wall and a window.

Perhaps he was in a room of some kind?

The walls of this room were fuzzy, and they beat in and out, like they had a pulse.

"Ooooooh Gaaaawwwwd," the voice said. Corey thought it sounded female in nature.

He moved his head to the right. He was able to tell at least that this was the direction from which the voice was coming. It was the girl he'd met the night before, before he'd met the Joker, but he couldn't remember her name.

"They got you in your sleeeeeeeeeeeeeeeeeeeep," the voice said, and then he saw the girl's lips move, but not until after he had heard the words spoken in their entirety. "Oh Gaaaaawwwwd."

The girl, who was now dressed in normal clothes, not in a dingy bathrobe like she had been in the day before, and like the one Corey was wearing now, picked up a suitcase and turned to leave. And then he heard the voice again. "Gooooood byyyyyyeeee."

"You should eeeeeaaaaaat soooooooome thiiiiing," another voice came now from the other direction. He looked to his left and saw his nemesis the Joker.

Corey felt his heart jump at the sight of the thing and its crazed smile, but at least it wasn't wearing makeup this time. He thought that might at least mean that he was awake and not dreaming, but being awake had never felt so much like a dream before. Not even in Iraq when he was coming off the crack that Dr. Feelgood was giving him and all of his battle buddies.

The Joker smiled again, and Corey blacked out.

When he came back out of the fog, at least a little, he was sitting in a chair across from Byron Blevins. Blevins' voice wasn't as slow as the other voices seemed before. It was speeding up a little, sounding as if someone was playing with the speed dial of an old 45 record player. Corey was among the last generation of Americans to see such archaic technology in regular use and hadn't thought about it in nearly thirty years until this moment.

"I seeeee you haaaave a suuuuuun," Blevins was saying. "IIIII dooooon't haaaave kiiiiiids myyyyyseeeelf. My wiiiiiife and IIII aren't quiiiiiiite reeeeaaady yet. Weeee're oooonly fooorty twoooo and sheeeee juuuuuuuuuust goooooooot heeeer Peeee AAAAAACH Deeeeeee."

And then Corey blacked out again.

"Beeeeee wuuuuuuun," the next voice said. He opened his eyes upon hearing it and found himself back in the conference room. The skinny lady with peppered hair from karaoke night, the night before, was back in front of the room with a bunch of little balls in a hamster cage.

Corey looked down at the table in front of him, and he saw his hands trembling like an alcoholic's in bad need of a drink and hovering over a card with a bunch of numbers and letters on it. The letters at the top of the card were pulsating like the walls of the room had been that morning.

"Yooouuu haaaave thaaat wuuuun buuuudy," the Joker said and then put a little green disk on the number 'one' on the card in front of him. Corey saw three disks and three number ones.

And then he blacked out again.

And then the Joker was waking him in the middle of the
night with the little salmon colored pill the size of a lime
seed and shaped like a football and then he blacked out again
and then he was sitting in the room with the fuzzy pulsating
walls and the Joker was there and someone was rapping about
pulling a trigger and someone else who talked like he had shit
in his mouth was accusing him of being racist because he wasn't
of the proper skin tone to say the "N" word and get away with it
and then he blacked out and then he was listening to Blevins go
on and on about something stupid he had researched about
Pavlov's dog and re-instating new stimuli and about how some big
dumb university was going to give him a Ph.D. for that and then
he blacked out again and then it was table golf night and in
spite of the fog Corey set a new ward record for making nine
holes in only fifteen strokes and the pepper haired skinny lady
was elated and promised to give him extra special compliments on
his chart and then he blacked out again and then he came to with
a start and thought he saw someone that looked like Jesus but
was black peek in the door and then leave and then the Joker was
waking him up again and by now he'd eaten enough of the little
salmon colored pills to see that the Joker had Tinker Bell with
him and she was flying just off to the right of his head when he
came in and he took another pill and then he blacked out and
then he was in the room with the pulsating walls again…

And this was his life for the next twenty eight days.

*Meeting between Jennifer Hutton (L.C.S.W.) and Corey Prine,
January 27, 2010

"Oh! My! God!" Jennifer said as two orderlies and the
asshole medic from before (Corey didn't notice a single thing
he'd said on the ride back to Beckley) walked Corey into her
office and sat him in the seat across from her.

"Sign here, Ma'am," the medic said, handing Jennifer the
clipboard he'd been carrying, as if Corey were a package being
delivered via U.P.S., and then he spit into his Go-Mart big gulp
cup.

"Thanks," she said, handing the clipboard back. "I think."
The orderlies and the medic left the room, but the medic looked
back before shutting the door and said, "Man, I bet he seen
lots'a shit!"

"What did they do to you, Corey?" Jennifer asked.

"It was the 'skittles.'"

"What?"

"The Joker and his 'skittles,'" he said, and then he
laughed and drooled. "But hey, at least I didn't see black
Jesus, I don't think." Then he laughed again.

Jennifer pulled up his file. She searched for the list of
meds that Corey had been given while he was on the psych ward in
Salem. She couldn't find it so she picked up the phone and
dialed 'the ward' down in Salem.

"Byron?" she said when the man picked up the phone and said 'hello' in a voice she still recognized. It was a voice that bore more apathy than just about any other she'd ever heard.

"Hi Jen," he said.

"What the hell were you guys feeding Corey Prine down there?"

"Oh, didn't you see the charts?"

"No," she said. "They aren't online."

"Oh," he said. "I must have neglected to send them. Sorry, I'll send them now. Is your screen up?"

"Yes," she said.

"Ok," he said, and Jennifer could hear him click clacking on his keyboard. "There you go."

"What the hell is DX-10?" she asked, incredulous.

"Oh, it's something new," Blevins said. "Nothing to worry about. It's in the same family as Xanax. A tranquilizer. We've found that it works quite well with patients such as Mr. Prine who have anger issues."

"Tranquilizer! Well, he's certainly tranquilized!" Jennifer shouted into the phone. She looked across her desk and saw Corey staring at his hands. Upon closer inspection she noticed that he was playing with the drool dangling from his lips. "Why didn't you consult me on this, Byron?"

"Hey," he said, very nonchalantly, "When you guys send 'em to us, we just assume they're out of your control and that you've done all that you can do for 'em, so we give 'em whatever we got down here that we think can help."

"He's a fucking Zombie!" she shouted, and Corey didn't even look up.

"I doubt he's going to beat the hell out of any more public servants," Blevins said, and she could hear the sarcasm in his voice. It was unlike Blevins. Sarcasm took effort. Perhaps he was reaching burn out with the VA?

"You aren't getting any more of my vets!" she screamed and then hung up the phone.

"Oh Corey," she said, sympathetically. "What are we going to do with you, Corey?"

"Got anymore 'skittles?'" he asked, finally looking up through glazed eyes.

*From the Personal diary of Jennifer Hutton- January 27, 2010

Dearest Diary,

Dear God, what have I done? I sent Corey Prine to Salem, thinking that a bit of inpatient treatment would help him. Especially in the eyes of the judge he'll have to stand before for beating the hell out of Rob. And no, I don't feel too bad for Rob.

Karma, I call it.

But Corey came back from Salem as a fucking Zombie! That worthless idiot Byron Blevins got his system filled with some tranquilizer called DX-10. I looked it up and found that, no, it *isn't* just like Xanax. It's just like Opium!

It's yet *another* trial drug by another ginormous pharmaceutical company we have a contract with, and they are using these guys as guinea pigs. Surprise, surprise Jen!

Are you really surprised?

Corey couldn't even stand on his own. I called his parents and they came and got him and took him home. Salem had sent him back with a couple bottles of this crap, but I told his parents not to give it to him, and to flush it down the toilet.

And burn the bottles.

I'm sure there is one hell of a street value for this stuff already (yes Dearest Diary, shit does fly out of the VA hospitals to the streets that fast) and I don't want some junkie digging around in his parent's trash bins at night and finding the bottles. They'll rob the house for sure!

I hope he can come off of this stuff with little trouble, but I doubt it. Looks like paranoia, depression, hostility and forgetfulness will be the flavors of the week, or ten to fourteen days, while he is coming down from this. Just like Xanax AND Opium, but to a much greater effect. And who the hell knows what else he'll go through, with this drug being so new and untested.

And I'm on my own now with Corey. Poor Jerry Barnes, God rest his soul. I'm still shocked at all he told me on our last meeting, but I know he was telling me for a purpose. Perhaps for a challenge I'll soon face but to which I may or may not be able to rise.

And to think, for all that Dr. Barnes did in and for his field and for all of *us* in the field. In spite of his secrets, which the little jury in my head is still collaborating on- as far as if what he had done was right or wrong, there were less than two dozen people at his funeral and I just think that that isn't right. If he hadn't been banned there would have been television crews there.

But he helped me, and I'm grateful.

And I know that in the end, his end, he was still helping me, trying to prepare me to face a decision that I hope I never have to face.

There's that word again, hope. It always seems to pop up when my gut is telling me something that my head doesn't want to hear.

S.O.S., Dearest Diary.

S.O.S.

20

*Meeting at the public defender's office at Summers County Courthouse, 125 Ballengee Street, Hinton, West Virginia, between Corey Prine, his parents, Jennifer Hutton, L.C.S.W. and Mr. Edward G Peyton, Esq. February 3, 2010

"Thanks for coming on short notice," Edward G. Peyton, the Summers County public defender said to everyone in attendance in the small, dank room in the basement of the Summers County Court House. "So, Mr. Peterson," he said, fumbling through the files spread out before him on the table that appeared to be older than the courthouse itself.

"Prine," Jennifer said, and then rolled her eyes. *This guy must be a long lost cousin of Byron Blevins, she thought.*

"Yes," he said, and then he dropped the file he'd been holding to the floor and the papers that had been in it fell out and scattered everywhere. "Prine," he said, taking the next file from the pile and ignoring everything that had fallen. "And you are Miss Hutton, correct?"

"Yes."

"And Mr. Prine," he said, facing toward Corey's father. "I have your permission to discuss the details of your case with Miss Hutton?"

"The other Mr. Prine," Corey's father said, pointing toward his son.

Everyone looked at Corey, who may have been in the room with them physically, but was certainly somewhere else in his head- far away in withdrawal land.

His face was ruddy, there were sweat beads all over his forehead and upper lip, and he couldn't control his hands. He alternated between rubbing them through his unkempt hair and on the thighs of his pants.

"Corey," Jennifer said, reaching over and touching him on the shoulder. He almost fell out of his chair in fright.

"Huh?"

"You're lawyer asked you if it is ok if I sit in on these proceedings with you, and listen to all the information discussed about your case."

"Is it?" Corey asked, as if *he* were the one who needed *her* permission.

"That's up to you, Corey."

"Sure, sure," he said and then turned his head to stare out the window in the top part of the wall of the basement. It was snowing heavily outside, and the weatherman on WBOY TV 4 news had warned of a hell of a snow storm that was coming.

"Ok," Mr. Peyton began. "I talked to the prosecutor. I tried to get us a plea of sorts but he isn't budging. He is going for a trial case, and he is going to ask for the maximum penalty of ten years incarceration after Mr. Prine is convicted."

"You sound so sure of yourself," Jennifer said.

"Excuse me?" he said, looking up with his eyebrows raised, attempting to give an impression of competence.

"You make it sound like Corey has no defense," she said.

"He doesn't," he said, and then he slid Rob the teller's medical records across the table to her. "He almost killed the guy. How do you defend that?"

"He has severe P.T.S.D.," she said. "He was acting while in a P.T.S.D. blackout!"

"Then," he said, digging through his files. "Can you explain this?" He slid a photocopy of Corey's denial of VA benefits across the desk. "According to your own people, he's perfectly healthy."

"Shit!" Jennifer said, without even looking at the denial letter she'd seen before.

"But you work with him," Corey's mother said, looking over at Jennifer. "Can't you do something?"

"Yes," Jennifer said. "I can write a letter of recommendation to the judge. And I can get the other medical professionals who have worked with Corey to do the same. I mean, he just spent a month on the ward in Salem. People without severe psychological issues don't get locked up on psych wards."

"Too late," Peyton said. "I tried that. The prosecutor said he knows its common practice for people to go inpatient somewhere, especially vets, once they've gotten themselves into trouble. He keeps coming back to this denial of claims form, saying there's no difference between Mr. Prine and the common man on the street, so therefore he should receive no special favors."

"No difference?" Corey said, joining the group now. "No difference? How much time did you spend in Iraq, mother fucker?"

"There's no need to be angry with me, Mr. Prine," Peyton said. "I'm on your side, remember?"

"You're on my side? Like the D.M.V.? Like the people of this grateful fucking nation? Like my goddam government?"

"Calm down, Corey," Jennifer said, reaching over and touching him on the shoulder. "Come on now, I want you to think your way through the fog. You're going through withdrawal from that crack Blevins put you on. You're angry. Just breathe."

"Yeah," the lawyer said. "And they always act like hard asses in the beginning. If I keep going back, he'll eventually cave. You'll probably see no more than a year in prison. Maybe six months with some probation tacked on to it. And you'll have to pay restitution. Whatever the guy's insurance didn't cover." He looked down at the table before speaking again. "But of course, he'll sue you in civil court. That *is* the American way, you know. He won't get anything, but be prepared to lawyer up again. And it won't be free because it's civil."

"Fuck you!" Corey said, rising to his feet and pointing at the lawyer. "And fuck the prosecutor and the civil courts and the fucking American way and everything else!"

And then he stormed out of the room.

"Corey!" Jennifer said as she rose to go after him. His parents sat in shock and Edward G. Peyton, Esq. began digging through his files in preparation for his next appointment.

"That went well," he said. "Glad I could help you folks out."

*

"Where are you going, Corey?" Jennifer said, grabbing him by the arm when she reached him in the hallway.

"Home!" he said. "I don't need to sit here and listen to this shit!"

Corey stomped up the stairs as his parents drew up beside Jennifer in the hallway.

"Keep an eye on him," she said. "If he goes anywhere, call me, and call the police. But call the police first."

"What do you think is going to happen?" his mother asked. Jennifer turned and looked the woman in the eyes. She saw the fear, the pain. Was that how her *mother's* eyes had looked a generation before?

"I don't know," Jennifer said. "I'm sorry, but I just don't know."

Corey went home and locked himself in his bedroom above his parent's garage. He blasted the heavy metal he loved to listen to when he was pissed off and sat in his bed.

But only for a minute, because he was going through withdrawal and it sucked and he was *so* pissed off that he needed something to improve his attitude, so he smoked a big fat bowl of marijuana and ate a handful of pills from the first bottle of pills he grabbed and then he ate a handful from each of the other bottles of pills from the VA, and by now he had quite the collection.

His own private pharmacy.

*

Jennifer had all intentions of going back to the VA for the rest of her appointments after leaving the courthouse, but on her way there her plans changed. She called her assistant and told her to reschedule her one o'clock, and that she was sure she would be there by two o'clock.

She turned her car around at a wide spot disguised as a used car lot. She noticed the proprietor inside asleep at his desk when she glanced over her shoulder to make sure that the coast was clear. She spun rocks pulling out of the parking lot and drove back onto the road, into the snow, and then straight for Rob's house just outside of town heading in the other direction on old route three toward Talcott.

"Shit!" the proprietor of the car lot said, half raising his sleepy head in time to see glowing taillights fading in the snow.

"Missed another sale!"

*

"Well, it's about time you came by and checked up on me," Rob said when he opened the door, surprised by Jennifer's presence. He had not seen her since before Christmas. "Come in. It's as cold as blue blazes and snowing like hell out there."

"No thank you," she said. "And I'm not here for you. I'm here for Corey Prine."

"What the *fuck* does he have to do with anything?"

"I want you to drop the charges, Rob. That's all you need to know."

"Fuck that! Look at me!" he said, pointing to his face. The bruises were gone but his nose was still crooked and swollen in the middle. "I can't fucking cough without almost crying with these fucking ribs," he said, pointing to his side. "I want that little fuck sitting on his ass in a prison cell for the next fucking decade, thinking about what he's done."

"He's already thinking about enough, Rob! And none of it has *anything* to do with you! You have no idea what this guy has gone through. First in Iraq, and now that he's back. All he wanted to do was get his goddam driver's license so he could get a fucking job and start falling back into life at home. But you had to be a fucking asshole, and you got your ass kicked, and I'm glad. Now, he's had enough. Drop the fucking charges!"

Rob smiled and gave her a once over. "I haven't had any pussy in a while," he said. "What say you come on in my trailer here, and let's see if we can't work something out in the form of a trade?"

Jennifer punched him in the nose so fast that he never saw it coming. Though she'd never struck another human being in her life, she managed to land the punch square on and re-brake his nose.

Rob dropped to his knees in agony. As he tried to catch the blood pouring from his nose which was making the snow on his porch turn purple, Jennifer said, "Fuck you, Rob!" and walked off of the porch and to her car.

When she reached her car, she told him to never call her or come by, or expect to see her ever again except for in court as a character witness for Corey Prine, and that he could feel free to have charges pressed against her as well.

But she knew he wouldn't press charges because Rob the teller was a redneck, and he would never want it to become public knowledge that a girl had kicked his ass.

She got in her car and drove back to the VA and worked out the rest of the day. And then, on her way to the gym, she got a call from Corey's mother.

"Jennifer!" she said. "Oh my God, Jennifer! You have to come back to Hinton! Corey's gone and he's taken a gun!"

22

The first shots rang out into the night and through the front window of Kirk's Bar and Grill on the Hinton bypass. It was a Tuesday, and just after 'supper time' as it's known by in West 'by God' Virginia. Business was slow, and the only two customers in the bar were Fred and Tina Foster. They'd been discussing whether or not they should take in their two young grandchildren to raise full time or get their precious daughter Lucy and her deadbeat husband Tony to go back to rehab, and figure out how to make it stick this time.

They heard the glass break and then looked up above their heads and noticed two bullet holes in the picture of the golf course from over at that fancy resort in Glade Springs (twenty holes now instead of eighteen) and then they waved to the barkeep, their other daughter, Sarah, and told her to bring them two more boiler-makers, and to put it on their tab.

When the police arrived they were just in time to hear shots ring out from the area of the Exxon out on Greenbrier Drive. Deputy number one told deputy number two to go into the bar and check for damages while he and deputy number three, who was just pulling up behind them, went to the Exxon.

*

James Henderson had just gotten out of his early model Ford Bronco in front of the little store at the Exxon to stock up on the necessities of the now raging snow storm; bread, milk and beer. Exxon charged a premium over the local grocery store, but they'd already sold out.

And all James really needed was more beer. He'd only *claimed* to have forgotten the bread and milk earlier. He had kept these snow storm staples hidden under the passenger seat of the Bronco. And he had to, because otherwise, his lovely bride of thirteen years, Angela, would not have let him out of the house for more beer.

He'd been leaning over the driver's seat, his door held wide open by the wind, digging the hidden goods out from under the passenger seat when the un-sensed bullet whizzed over his head and shattered the glass of the passenger side window. He stood up, looked behind him, and then seeing no one, turned and looked through the broken glass.

"Goddam!" he said. "Cold enough to break glass out here!"

And then he staggered into the Exxon and bought another case of Schlitz.

*

While Jennifer was racing back on old route three, almost through Shady Spring, her cell phone rang, and she recognized the number.

"Corey!" she said. "Where are you? What's going on?"

"I've had enough," he said. She could hear the wind howling through the cell phone.

"Where are you?" she asked. "Corey, please."

"I'm here," he said. "Outside."

"Outside where?"

"Outside of my body."

"Corey. You are going through some badass withdrawal! Can you just sit tight until I get there? Are you somewhere safe?"

"I'm so cold," he said.

"Are you outside? I hear the wind. God, Corey, where are you?"

"I'm here."

"Where is here?" she said, pleading, taking the turns even faster now, in spite of the snow that covered the road. The plows had been through earlier, but this was West Virginia, where snow plows were more for decoration than practicality. There *was* no practical way to deal with winter in West Virginia, other than to stay inside and wait it out. She hoped she'd even be *able* to make it to Hinton with these conditions.

"I can look down and see myself," he said. His voice sounded like he was in a trance.

"What do you see?" She was trying to buy time. Keep him on the line.

"I see myself," he said.

"And what do you look like?" she said.

"I don't look like me," he said.

"Why not, Corey?"

"That's not my weapon," he said.

"What? Corey! Do you still have the gun?"

"It's not my weapon," he said again. "It's Emerson's."

"Corey! Just stay exactly where you are until I get there," she said.

"But they'll come for me," he said. "And I can't let them take me! And this isn't my weapon. It's Emerson's. I can see it. I'm right down there holding it. In the water."

"Corey, please. Just listen to me." Pleading now like she never had with anyone.

"What do I do?" he asked, sounding like a lost child reaching out to a parent in the dark; a parent who had abandoned him, or who had never accepted him in the first place.

"Corey," she said, and then took a long pause. "There is only one thing you *can* do."

"What was that?" he asked. "The storm. I can't hear you. You're breaking up on me. What did you say?"

And then she heard him mumble, 'Damn, I'm looking up at myself. With Emerson's weapon.'

"There is only one thing you can do, Corey," she said again.

And then the phone went dead.

*

The cops fishtailed off of Greenbrier Drive and onto the Willowwood-Wiggins Bridge that crossed the New River and lead to old, county route thirteen. They were able to come to a stop on the bridge just in time, before running over the body of the former Corey Prine, age 28, E-4 Specialist and Iraq War Vet, machine gunner- Mosul 2008-2009.

Postscript:

*-Formal charges were not brought, and disciplinary actions were not taken against Jennifer Hutton by the Department of Veterans Affairs, mostly at the pleading of Corey Prine's parents. After the interrogation, she took an indefinite leave of absence.

She returned to Bellevue, Washington and began work on her Ph.D. at her Alma mater, the University of Washington, the focus of her thesis being Mental Health Administration.

She plans to someday return to work for the Department of Veterans Affairs, but as an administrator, not a councilor- her goals being to eliminate red tape and change procedure- make the organization's primary focus the treatment of veterans and not the clearing of claims.

And to prevent veterans from being used as lab rats by the large pharmaceutical firms who hold contracts with the U.S. Government.

She has begun a conscientious lobbying group, pushing for tort reform in the mental health industry, in the hopes that counselors and psychiatrists can someday again focus on the best interests of their patients without fear of legal repercussions when things work out differently than everyone involved had hoped; shift the focus back to the veterans and civilian mental health patients who need help, instead of upon whom to place blame when things go wrong.

Though she found it surprisingly easy to convince her interrogators during the VA inquiry after Corey Prine's suicide that what she had meant by, "There is only one thing you can do," was 'to lay down your gun and surrender to authorities,' she has had a difficult time convincing herself that that was what she had meant.

She could remember, during the call, that she could not hear any static that Corey had claimed to hear on *his* end of the line. In spite of the storm, the line sounded perfectly clear.

When she listened to the replay of the call during the interrogations, she had felt chills run up her spine as she realized that the line had indeed been clear.

Even in his crazed state of mind, Corey Prine had kept her from having to make the decision she'd been struggling with since her last meeting with Dr. Jerry Barnes. She hoped she would never be in a situation to have to face such a decision again, and she wanted to do all that she could to assure the same for other mental healthcare providers. She would be forever grateful to Corey.

She and her mother are enjoying their time together and have become closer than they've ever been. They visit her father's grave at Lake View Cemetery on Capitol Hill in Seattle once a month and on Veteran's Day every November.

*- Rob (the former teller) filed a personal injury suit against the West Virginia Division of Motor Vehicles, his lawyers claiming he was beaten due to a lack of proper security provided for employees. They settled out of court for a publicly undisclosed amount.

An amount that got bigger and bigger, according to Rob, with the more beer that he drank.

All of the money was gone in six months. He'd spent it mostly on bar hopping around Raleigh County telling war stories. The more he drank, the better the stories. By the time he was broke, he was up for the Congressional Medal of Honor.

Even though he'd never deployed.

*- The estate of Dr. Jerry Barnes was split evenly between his two lovely assistants, Anna and Mina. His estranged son, La Verne, a '*fucking*' lawyer in Northern West Virginia, filed suit to no avail.

La Verne, in his sixties at the time of his father's death, had led a much checkered career, and even by this stage of his career, could not afford to pay for a legal assistant to work in his home office (he couldn't afford the rent downtown). He kept filling the suit filing forms out incorrectly, and the judge kept rejecting them.

He eventually gave up and went back to practicing law, pro-bono, where he continued making very little money, being that thirty percent of nothing is nothing.

   -*Anna used a portion of her inheritance to buy a small house in Beckley, West Virginia and a new car in which she could commute to classes at Mountain State University where she began work to obtain a nursing degree. She earned a 4.0 G.P.A. during her first two semesters, and then had to transfer to Marshall University in Huntington without getting credit for her classes that she'd completed because of the closing of Mountain State University due to lack of accreditation.

   -*Mina took her money and returned to her homeland, the Philippine Islands, where her large immediate and extended family helped her spend her inheritance in less than a year, in spite of the currency conversion heavily favoring the U.S. dollar; 42 to 1.

   The money was spent mostly on pig roast parties were the local, rot-gut, Tanduay Rum, and extremely strong Red Horse beer (7% alc. per volume-and which *does* contain actual horse urine) flowed freely until her funds were gone. She has since returned to the United States and has begun work, again, as a caregiver for geriatrics. And though no one in her family has come to help her wipe asses and change adult diapers, she still continues to send most of her earnings home to them.

   -*Byron Blevins resigned in the middle of the "Black Jesus" investigation at the VA hospital in Salem, Virginia. Evidence had been gathered, suggesting that illegal lobotomies had been performed on certain patients. It is yet to be determined who was behind the lobotomies, why they were performed, and why they were able to go on undetected for so long.

   Blevins was deemed 'too inept to have anything to do with such an elaborate scheme' by investigators and was cleared.

   He considered the investigator's findings on his behalf a compliment.

   He has since become the guidance counselor at Richland High School in Richland, Kentucky and as of yet, still has not finished his thesis and been awarded a Ph.D.

*-Pete Richards has allegedly been spotted bouncing back and forth between the southernmost Islands of the Philippines and the northernmost islands of Indonesia. It has been rumored that he is doing some sort of undisclosed contract work for the Philippine Army, helping them weed out terrorists from the various terrorist groups in the region, including Abbu Sayyaf, MILF, and the NPA.

One of his former NCO's, *then* Staff Sergeant White, now Sergeant First Class, retired, White, has gone looking for him in attempts to bring him back.

Re-patriot the patriot.

-*Within the passing of one year of Corey Prine's suicide, two more soldiers that had served under, *then,* LT Bee in Mosul had committed suicide. Three are currently serving prison terms for violent crimes, three for crimes pertaining to illegal drug use, and four are currently receiving intense, inpatient care (and some really trippy meds) on any of the various 'wards' scattered throughout the U.S.'s vast system of VA hospitals.

More complaints were filed with the Inspector General, mostly by family members of the suffering and deceased vets. An investigation was launched, and Captain Bee was summarily promoted to *Major* Bee. With a small portion of the pay raise that came with his rank promotion, he purchased the entire series of 'Prison Fights' on dvd.

-*Corey Prine is *finally* at peace.

Afterward:

Though "Off Switch" is a work of fiction, it is based on fact; events that my battle buddies from my former Washington Army National Guard unit and I faced while on deployment in Iraq, and issues some of us have faced since returning.

I am now, and forever will be pro-soldier. My time spent in the military gives me some of the fondest memories of my life.

Yet also some of the most disturbing.

I want to point out some of the 'unbelievable' accounts in this novel that are based on real events.

During *my* first four months in Iraq I did NOT receive pay, and my National Guard leadership, through my chain of command, did nothing. My platoon leader, a certain lieutenant, would NOT allow me to simply go to the finance office and inquire about my pay problem.

When I pleaded with this lieutenant to allow me to do so, as my three children back in the states were going without their needs being met because I was not paying my child support as a result of not receiving my bi-weekly paycheck while I was deployed to a warzone, he told me, "Lake, you don't know how good you and your kids have it. You need to look at these kids in Iraq and realize how lucky you and your kids are."

And then he told me that if I were to go to the finance office I would be reprimanded, placed on extra duty, and would 'fill every sandbag he could find in Mosul.'

Only when I was on my way to complain to the Inspector General, again, four months after not having been paid, was I finally escorted to the finance office by my First Sergeant. We were able to get my pay problem resolved **that day**. My First Sergeant told me he would have done so sooner, but the lieutenant had been telling him that my problem was already fixed and not to worry about it.

And I know my First Sergeant was telling the truth.

But the damage had been done. My ex-wife had made arrangements to move my three children to England, against my knowledge, during this period, and I didn't have a legal leg to stand on since I had not been supporting my family .

While I was later hospitalized (for 6 months!) upon return from my deployment, she did in fact move my children to England. I went to J.A.G. seeking legal help, and they told me they wouldn't help me because the Army couldn't appear to look anti-family in the eyes of the media and the public by getting involved in such family sensitive cases.

I have seen my children three times in the three years since.

*

Members of my unit and I were denied permission, by our National Guard leadership, to receive medical attention for injuries we sustained while we were in Iraq. We were threatened with reprimands, article 15's and loss of rank and pay, for 'malingering' (faking injury or illness) by our leadership.

One of my battle buddies broke one of his fingers while playing basketball during one of our forced P.T. sessions between missions. When he finally sought medical treatment in spite of the threats from our leadership, he was taken off of mission for a couple of weeks so his finger could heal, understandably and only because of doctor's orders, but then assigned extra duty by our leadership as punishment for seeking medical attention.

We really *were* forced by our National Guard leadership to take mandatory P.T. tests while we were in theater. I had never scored below the perfect 300 mark in my career, but I was forced to take these tests as well while many of those among our senior leadership, N.C.O.s who held squad leader and platoon sergeant positions, and who hadn't passed a P.T. test in years ('pencil whipping' the results from their National Guard Unit offices before turning the results in to National Guard Headquarters) did not.

On one such exam, after an extended convoy security mission, something in my groin region snapped, and hurt like hell while I was doing sit-ups.

And then I was forced to run two miles, for time.

I walked and worked and continued to go on missions hunched over and in pain for the remainder of the deployment, because I was denied permission by my National Guard leadership to seek medical treatment for my injury.

With less than two weeks to go in theater and only after our unit had been replaced on missions by the new incoming unit, I finally sought medical treatment, against the permission of my leadership, and was misdiagnosed with a hernia.

When we returned to the states, I was stationed at the Warriors in Transition Battalion (WTB- medical holdover unit for wounded soldiers) at Fort Lewis, just south of Seattle, Washington, where it was found that I had actually disconnected my epididymis. In laymen's terms, the tube that connects to the testicle and carries seminal fluid to the outside world had been torn off of my right testicle. I apologize to those of you with weak stomachs, but that is what happened and there is no simpler way to state it.

I spent the next six months in the hospital having surgery and being treated for a severe infection caused by seminal fluid having drained into my inguinal canal and spoiling. This is what caused the swelling and the pain in my groin region that gave all appearances of a hernia. All of this could have been treated in Iraq, in a matter of days, had I been allowed to seek medical treatment. I would not have suffered so much for so long and lost another six months of my life to the Army.

Also, I would have avoided the worst, which was yet to come.

While I was on medical holdover, I got addicted to pain killers. Namely, Vicodin, but also whatever my battle buddies stationed at the WTB were willing to trade for my Vicodin. Narcotics were handed out to us like candy, and though I needed them dreadfully at first, due to the level of intensity to which the pain from my injury had progressed since I was denied medical attention by my leadership while in Iraq, there came a point where I no longer needed it, and I begged the doctors to quit prescribing it to me, as I've known my entire life that I have an addictive personality, and at times I have struggled with addiction. The idea of returning to active addiction and not being able to shake it again was scaring the hell out of me. They'd tell me 'not to be a tough guy' and give me a bottle of forty for the week, and I ate every damn last one of them, except for the ones I exchanged with other soldiers for other drugs.

I spent the next two years struggling with addiction.

*

Suicide was quite an issue at the WTB, but while I was there, there was only one.

I spent Christmas Day of 2010 with a soldier who would soon commit suicide. Though I'd been at the WTB for several months by then, and had seen this soldier around, I had never really spoken to him. He had been at the WTB for some time, nearly two years if memory serves me correctly, and had no expected date for when he was to leave.

One of his legs had been crushed during a recent deployment and it wavered back and forth between paralysis and recovery, as he explained it to me, but it seemed to be spending longer periods of time in a state of paralyses and less time among the living appendages of his body. He shared with me that he had been begging the Army to amputate his leg and allow him to learn to live with a prosthetic, and allow him to also get out of the WTB and get on with his life.

But they wouldn't.

A weak or so later, when we had our first formation after the New Year's break, this soldier was a no-show. The leadership went searching for him and found him sometime later in his room, dead from an overdose of his prescription medications. He had apparently been there, in his private room, for days, and no one had even checked on him.

On the day of the memorial service, I commented to one of our N.C.O.'s in charge at the WTB that it didn't seem real to me that I had eaten Christmas dinner with someone who was now dead because of suicide. I was wishing I could have seen a sign, that there was something I could have said or done. Then the N.C.O. said to me, "It's about time he killed himself. We've been telling him to just kill himself for a while now."

As you can imagine, I was shocked. I asked this N.C.O. what they meant and they told me that they used to have this soldier in their platoon and had requested he be transferred because he was always 'crying about killing himself,' and that this N.C.O. and others were 'sick of hearing it, and had been telling him to just do it and get it over with.'

He finally did.

*

My driver's license really had expired while I was in Iraq and when I attempted to renew them in West Virginia, my home state and to where I had relocated not long after being released from the hospital, I was unable to do so. But this was not because of any 'dick measuring contest' with anyone at the W.V. D.M.V. The people there were very kind and helpful (because that's how Mountaineers roll!) and helped me find a contact number to the D.M.V. in Virginia, the state in which my license had been previously held.

It turned out that they *did* have a hold on my license because I had allowed my auto insurance to expire while I was in Iraq. But it was on a truck that I really had relieved myself of during the deployment. I *did not* own it anymore when the insurance lapsed.

They told me that my DD-214 would NOT work for proof of my deployment, and that I needed to get the C.O. of my National Guard unit to send them a certified letter stating that I had been with them in Iraq during the disputed dates, or otherwise pay a nearly $600 fine for not having insurance.

I contacted my old National Guard unit in regard to this matter, and a week later they got back in touch with me and told me that they needed a certified letter from the Virginia D.M.V. requesting a certified letter from them.

Seriously!

I've since relocated to the Philippine Islands, a nation of which I am not a citizen, and have never fought in a war to defend (though my forefathers have liberated them twice in the last 120 years, first from Spain in the Spanish American War and then from Japan in WWII), and I have had no problems buying a motorcycle here, getting it registered, insured, and licensed and driving at will. Yet when I left America to come here, two years after having returned from deployment to Iraq, I still had not been granted a driver's license to drive on the roads of the nation of which I had been sent to Iraq to defend. I was still waiting on certified letters from two different government agencies who were busy passing the buck back and forth.

Where the hell is Harry Truman when you need him?

*

I still reside in the Philippines and am happy to report, that as of the writing of this book, I have beaten addiction again, or rather, have been given a daily reprieve from the terrifying grasps of addiction.

For today.

And those daily reprieves have been stacking up. It has been nearly a year since I have eaten any of the 'skittles' given me by the Army hospital at Ft. Lewis, or any of the seven, that is correct, seven different prescription medications given me by the VA hospital in Beckley, WV.

I did suffer from chronic pain while in the U.S. as a result of injuries I sustained while in Iraq (that goddam body armor) and the colder temperatures, but the tropical environment of the Philippines allows me to live relatively pain free without the use of drugs that put me in more of a hell than any physical pain I've ever experienced; drugs that hijack my mind and make it impossible for me to think straight, or in any way be a productive member of any society.

All that the drugs seemed to enable me to do was take more drugs. I certainly was not able to write while on them, let alone live life the way it is meant to be lived, the way I am living it today.

*

At this point in time, the largest battle the U.S. military faces is not on some far away battlefield in the Middle East, but within its own ranks. Broken and disturbed soldiers, who are angry, depressed, and confused, are killing themselves in historical record numbers.

For the first time in world history, more soldiers from a certain war or wars, (the wars in the Middle East) have died from suicide than have died on the battlefield.

And the National Guard and Army Reserve suicide numbers are not even being included among the Army suicide rate numbers being given to the public!

Smarter men and women than me are addressing the issue, and for the sake of my brothers and sisters in arms, I hope they figure it out. I might offer a few simple suggestions, but as I was never anything more than a lower enlisted man (E-4 specialist) who never knew my place (according to my former National Guard leadership who didn't feel I was worthy of receiving pay to care for my family, or receive medical care when I was seriously and painfully injured), my views may not carry much weight, or even be very good, but here they are:

1-   When the war is over, go home. By the time my unit deployed to Iraq, we were simply occupying a defeated nation and everyone on both sides knew it. So many vets have deployed, many of them repeatedly, merely to spend a year of their lives escorting and protecting civilian contractors who are piling up profits selling the U.S. Army and foreign governments anything from concrete to soda-pops, while their personal lives are falling to pieces back home.

Yes, we enlisted. We volunteered. But it was to fight a threat against America, and to defend others in foreign lands who do not possess the ability to defend themselves, not to watch publicly traded companies increase quarterly profits consistently to please shareholders, or to suffer at the hands of abusive, toxic leadership who develop prison mentalities, perhaps out of sheer boredom as much as anything else.

2-   Perhaps the men and women who have fought overseas should be allowed to seek medical and mental healthcare treatment in the private sector, beginning immediately upon returning from deployment, and then bill the Veterans Affairs Administration who seems, at times, too busy with red tape and protocol to provide timely care themselves.

Delay, deny and hope that I die?

If the private sector is good enough for the public, then why isn't it good enough for the troops? Especially when the military and government sides seems to have been able to do all they can in special cases ("…we've all been telling him to just kill himself," the N.C.O. said as we headed to the memorial service).

Less than one half of one percent of the American people ever serves in the U.S. armed forces. Less than half of those ever deploy, even during a time of war. These men and women deserve the best upon returning home, if they are fortunate enough to do so.

3- And finally, it has been noted that substance abuse is the second most common risk factor for suicide after major depression and bipolar disorder, and many people who suffer from P.T.S.D. also suffer from depression. So, add to a veteran's depression drug addiction, via the small, private pharmacies the VA is handing out to most veterans suffering from P.T.S.D., and especially those who suffer from any physical pain, and it is pretty easy to see, as I hope I have made painstakingly clear in this novel, that you end up with veterans now suffering from depression *and* drug addiction.

This adds up to suicide waiting to happen.

I'm not a doctor or a social worker, so I am not technically qualified to give advice in this regard, but after my own experiences I am certainly free to give my own opinion.

Not to mention, I spent a year in hell earning that right and giving everyone else the right to do the same.

*

I hope you've enjoyed "Off Switch" and I apologize for my little rant at the end. If you read it all, thank you for lending me your ear.

May God bless the American soldier and keep him safe from the enemy during times of battle and safe from each other during times of occupation.

And safe from himself once he returns home.

Other Books Available by Kevin E Lake

1- Homeless Across America (non-fiction)

http://www.amazon.com/Homeless-Across-America-ebook/dp/B004HB2484/ref

2- Serial Street

http://www.amazon.com/Serial-Street-ebook/dp/B004HFRLPQ/ref

3- From the Graves of Babes *

http://www.amazon.com/From-Graves-Babes-ebook/dp/B004N62RU8/ref

4- Isle of Kapre

http://www.amazon.com/Isle-Kapre-Kevin-Lake-ebook/dp/B00DJXXC0A/ref

*Amazon's #1 ghost novel in customer satisfaction for six months in the year of its release!

Want to know what became of Corey Prine's battle buddy from Iraq, Pete Richards? Read the latest full length novel by author and Iraq War veteran Kevin E Lake "Isle of Kapre."

"Isle of Kapre"

http://www.amazon.com/Isle-Kapre-Kevin-Lake-
ebook/dp/B00DJXXC0A/ref

After serving in Iraq and failing to reintegrate into American
society, Pete Richards expatriates to the Philippine Islands. As
he struggles with unraveling his emotions from the war, he also
struggles with integrating into Eastern culture, where what you
see is not always what you get, and warm and friendly smiles
from strangers are not always indicative of warm and friendly
intentions.

By the time Richards starts making sense of his new
surroundings, he's broke and he takes to mercenary work for
income, helping the Philippine Army track down members of the
various terrorist groups that plague the islands. During this
time he meets Rose, a beautiful Filipina who comes to him for
help, claiming that her younger sister has been kidnapped by the
terrorist network Abu Sayyaf. Hesitantly, he agrees to help when
she offers him a sum that he cannot refuse for his services.

Richards soon finds himself on a mysterious island with Rose,
the Isle of Kapre, where his views on what is real and what
isn't take another turn as they encounter mythical creatures and
beasts straight out of Philippine superstitions and folklore in
their attempt to find Rose's sister. Matters become worse when
he finds out that Rose is not exactly what she's claimed to be,
and when he learns the truth about her sister, who has been
taken by a force much darker and more powerful than any rag tag
group of hooligans.